Practically MAGIC

Practically MAGIC

Jen Calonita

HarperCollins Children's Books, a division of HarperCollins Publishers, 195 Broadway, New York, NY 10007

HarperCollins Publishers, Macken House, 39/40 Mayor Street Upper, Dublin 1, D01 C9W8, Ireland

Avon a is an imprint of HarperCollins Publishers.

Practically Magic

harpercollins.com

Library of Congress Control Number: 2026934650
ISBN 978-0-06-351764-6

Typography by Jessie Gang
26 27 28 29 CPI 10 9 8 7 6 5 4 3
FIRST EDITION

For Miana Delucia and Michelle Ragno
and road trips full of magic

Practically
MAGIC

1

Mystic Hollow Community Page

NEW POST FROM PAGE ADMINISTRATOR:
Halloween is less than a week away! Comment below if you'll be welcoming trick-or-treaters and what candy kids can expect. (Tip: Get good candy. No shade, but we all remember Abe Henderson of Appletree Lane's Necco Wafers Fail of Halloween 2024.)

"Everyone grab a partner," Mr. Ruth says. "Remember, whoever comes up with the best Halloween display will have it featured in the town green! And yes, you'll get five extra points added to your lowest test score."

My best friend, Laney, steps up next to me, like she always does, but I subtly shake my head. Laney and I could totally crush this competition, and while I'm never one to say no to extra credit, right now there's something more important than that.

But that *something* is currently talking to Zara Patel. I'll have to move quickly if I want to be lab partners with him.

I've been waiting all month to find a time to ask Colton Croft to come to my Halloween party. The note that I passed him in history had a perfect message that was equal parts flirty and confident, but when Mrs. Hullman slammed the door, it went flying directly into the trash. When I tried waving him down in gym class, a tenth grader mistook my gesturing as an invitation to chuck the basketball at my head. Even once I was on the floor, Colton Croft didn't even look at me.

But this time, it's going to work. I'm going to get Colton Croft to notice me. We're going to crush this experiment, have it enshrined on the town green, and he's going to come to my Halloween party, where he'll realize that I'm the girl he's been looking for, and we'll get married and finally unite the two oldest families in Mystic Hollow.

I just need to get to the lab bench before Zara sits down next to him.

Colton is so cute, you'd think someone designed him on Canva. He's got expressive blue eyes, a strong jawline, and killer blond hair that I can picture running my fingers through. Plus, Colton is funny, charming, town royalty (his dad is mayor), and our star quarterback. Is it at all a surprise I'd been in love with him forever? Or, you know, technically a year?

"Don't tell me you're going for dry ice," a voice mutters behind me.

"Get out of my way, Powell," I bite back. The last thing

I need is Zach Powell blocking me here as well. He's been a tenth of a GPA point ahead of me all year, thanks to taking a second language as a senior—of course he's going to score straight A's at freshman-level French.

But the extra time spent swerving around Zach—who happens to be infuriatingly tall—is all it takes. Zara slips onto the stool beside Colton.

"Katherine," Mr. Ruth says. "Who's your partner?"

"I—" I gesture toward Colton, who is helping Zara put on her goggles. She giggles. I grit my teeth.

"I'll work with Kat," Zach offers.

"I'll work alone," I say at the same time.

Mr. Ruth frowns. "You need a lab partner. Two heads are better than one. We haven't had a student win on their own since . . . well, your sister."

Now I'm definitely not working with Zach.

"In fact," Mr. Ruth continues, raising his voice, "don't bother trying anything with dry ice. Harriet Hadley's exemplary display of sublimation two years ago—"

I snatch up the dry ice. Zach raises a brow at me. "Sure that's a good idea, Hadley?"

"Yes," I say shortly, stepping up to the only empty lab bench. Unfortunately, that means Zach has to follow me. He helps himself to a pair of goggles, tangling them in his curls as he tries to get them over his normal glasses. When he holds out a pair to me, they knock into my nose—I was staring at Colton again.

They seem to be making some sort of bright green slime. Zombie brains? Colton is laughing, flicking it toward Zara, who shrieks and tries to shield her curtain of long, dark hair.

"Mr. Ruth already said your sister did it best—"

I might growl at Zach. That might be the noise coming out of my mouth. While Laney would hold up her hands in defeat, Zach only glares right back at me.

"Need I remind you," I continue, digging in the drawer for a beaker. I'm not sure what I'll do with the dry ice that will be better than what my perfect sister did—considering Mr. Ruth is *still* extolling her Halloween display—but I need to do something better. "I won the science fair last year."

Zach folds his arms over his chest, blocking out the "FurReal" logo on his tee. It's the name of the animal rescue "initiative" he started at Mystic Hollow High this year. Not a club. An initiative. Apparently, it looks better on college applications. At least that's what I overheard him bragging to someone. I'm in five clubs—my sister was only in four—but I've never created one. I'm not sure that group silent reading sessions or candle making would look quite as impressive on my résumé, so what's the point?

"You won on a technicality," Zach goes on. "My tornadic activity experiment came in second by less than a tenth of a point." I snort. "Seriously, Hadley, we should do our own thing."

If he wants to go to battle, my armor is ready. "*We* are

not doing anything. Mr. Ruth just said we can enter on our own. My sister did it."

"You aren't Harry Hadley," Zach points out, and I rip the next drawer open so sharply that the beakers nearly break, hot anger scorching down my neck. Laney shoots me a concerned look from where she's paired up with Zach's old lab partner. I shake my head subtly, and she points over at Colton, who is "helping" Zara stir their slime from behind, his arms around her like a bear hug.

I could choke on my jealousy.

But then I notice where Laney is pointing. On the counter sits an orange envelope. Even from here, I can see Zara's flowing script: *Colton Croft <3*.

Laney mouths at me, "Invite?"

My stomach swoops. What if Zara Patel is having a Halloween party too? And if she invites Colton? And he says yes to her—and not to me?

It'll all be for nothing. My month of handcrafting decorations. All the times I've tried to convince my mom that I can safely host a party at our house. I even already sent all the invitations, personalized to every kid in my grade. This is the one year when I'm not in Harry's shadow, when my parents are going to be out of town.

I have to get Colton to my Halloween party.

I need to make sure Colton doesn't get that invitation.

Across the room, Laney is mouthing something I can't quite pick up on. Her lab partner gives her a strange look as she starts gesturing over her head, forming a tall triangle from her temples up, hands meeting two feet above her crown. As if she's wearing a giant pointy hat.

Right.

I may not be Harry Hadley, but I am *a* Hadley. And every Hadley girl is a witch. I can spell my way out of this. I gather my long red hair and use the hair tie on my wrist to pull it into a messy bun so I can focus. Of course I didn't get Harry's sleek blond locks.

Spell casting requires two things: intention and sacrifice. Spells work best if you sacrifice something that represents the target—in this case, it's easy, since the target is just a note. I rip a piece of paper from Zach's binder—he squawks at me, but I ignore him—and scribble my intention. *Destroy Zara's note.*

"We should work as a team," Zach is saying, cranking up his Bunsen burner. When he turns to double-check his chemicals—boric acid and alcohol, so he's going for a green flame, which is annoyingly clever—I lunge forward for the fire.

Sacrifice. If I burn this paper imbued with my meaning, the spell should work.

Emphasis on *should*. Because even though I'm a teenage witch from twenty generations of the most powerful witches, my spells rarely work as intended. To put it mildly.

Laney gives me a thumbs-up as I jerk my note toward the fire.

"Kat! Watch out!" Zach cuts in, trying to yank my hand away from the Bunsen burner. His obnoxiously large hand clamps over mine, hot and rough, but I shove my way forward. Rage burns through me at the way he manhandles me, but I try to focus on my intention. *Destroy*, I think, pushing the note into the flames.

The fire catches, and the little scrap of lined paper blackens, curls, and smokes.

Zach swears under his breath, knocking the ashes onto the black tabletop.

I ignore him and hold my breath, glancing over at Zara.

As Colton ducks down to dig through his bag, Zara perches on the lab stool, whisks her hair down her back, and opens her lab notebook with a flourish.

As the marbled black-and-white cover falls open, the pages glow, and my hands suddenly go numb and tingly. A split second and my stomach sinks with a realization. Zach lurches forward, tackling Zara to the floor, as the paper explodes in flames that shoot up five feet, a column of fire to the ceiling.

I yelp and reach for the fire extinguisher, coating the entire bench—and Zara and Zach—in foam. As my hands shake, my brain catches up.

Destroy Zara's note.

I wasn't clear enough. Apparently, I was enthusiastic about the *destroy* part, but maybe I hadn't thought clearly about which note—or notebook. My heart leaps into my throat. Does that mean the spell worked?

Then we hear a ghostly moan.

I scan the table and floor. Because as the smoke billows, I can't see Colton.

A figure staggers through the haze, hands out, and I follow the broad shoulders, hoping to see Colton's golden hair, his bright smile, his blue eyes.

Instead, I see nothing. Because this figure doesn't have a head.

"Oh my god! It's the Headless Horseman!" someone shouts. Lab stools clatter to the linoleum as people scatter. Tom Callabra, the biggest football player on the team, yelps and tries to use Laney as a human shield.

"Hey, man!" she complains, knocking him aside, but he's already sprinting toward the door, as Mr. Ruth tries to urge students to evacuate in a calm and orderly process.

Still, the figure lurches forward. Toward me.

It's a familiar shape that I've seen at our football games and emblazoned on Colton's jersey. But just because our mascot is the Headless Horseman doesn't mean I was prepared to see the actual Headless Horseman during third-period chemistry.

"Kat!" Laney says. "Do something!"

He's wearing all black with a long jacket and tails, and riding boots. The real clue we're in trouble is the fact the figure has no head. Just a collar with a severed neck peeking out of his shirt. Slowly the Horseman walks through the crowd that parts for him like the sea. Mr. Ruth steps forward, leveling his jaw.

"That is enough," he says. "Halloween costumes are only allowed on Halloween. And even then, only when you pay the five-dollar donation to the Horseman Scholarship Fund for seniors. Unmask yourself!"

A low moan issues from the headless figure, and he steps forward, hands shaking as they near Mr. Ruth's forehead, knocking glasses from his nose.

"I mean it!" I hear Mr. Ruth try once more, but his voice cracks as the Horseman lets out another ghostly moan.

"This is a job for Kat Hadley," Laney whispers. "Do something!"

I don't hesitate. I have to try. I look around wildly for an object I can imbue with my intention then destroy. What represents the Headless Horseman? A . . . head? Something with a face?

There's another scream. The Horseman has his arms around Zara. She swings her arms wildly to get away.

"Help me!" Zara cries. "Someone help me!"

"Do something!" Laney hisses again. "Before he drags all our spirits down to the underworld!"

Zara used to call me "Carrot Top" in elementary school, but I still don't want to see her join Hades before her time. But then it all clicks. Something orange that has a face. Or at least, can have a face—if you carve it. "Trying! I need a pumpkin." I lunge toward the front table, where Mr. Ruth laid out all the supplies for our Halloween displays. My hands are tingling again, like I've hit both funny bones at the same time.

My aunts are always telling me that I have the magic inside me—that I'm a Hadley, that it doesn't matter if Harry cast her first spell at three to call the biggest snowstorm Connecticut's ever seen and I still can't even conjure a single raindrop on purpose. But whenever I try to cast a spell, all I feel is panic. Empty, helpless panic.

Because I'm not Harry Hadley, and I'm not even sure if I deserve to be *a* Hadley.

"Pumpkin!" Laney says, chucking one at me.

I fumble for the gourd. I don't have time to write anything, so I'll have to just think extra hard. It's risky—Harry still writes most of her spells—but if I can pull this off, I'll be a hero. *Destroy the Horseman*, I tell it. And then I put it back down on the linoleum and attempt to smash the small pumpkin with my foot.

Instead, my ankle rolls, the pumpkin shooting out as if I've booted it for a corner kick.

"Uh-oh," Laney and I whisper as the pumpkin slams directly into Zach's foam-covered shin.

"Oww!" he cries.

That's when I hear someone laughing.

"Everyone chill!" Colton's voice comes from inside the Horseman, and I watch as he unzips the collar and reveals his own head. "It's just me." He shrugs out of his costume and shows off his sweaty self. The boy even looks good glistening. "Scared you good, didn't I?" he asks.

And then he turns directly at me and winks.

At me.

Slowly, the classroom quiets. Zach looks like he lost a fight with a giant toothpaste tube. The lab has fared far worse; I've seen less disastrous photos from the aftermath of earthquakes. Stools are scattered. Someone shattered an Erlenmeyer flask in their haste to escape. And everything is coated in foam.

Mr. Ruth is glaring from the charred remains of Zara's notebook to the lone Bunsen burner in the entire room that's lit. That's when the sprinklers kick in overhead, the fire alarm blaring.

Oh boy.

"What just happened?" Mr. Ruth demands, his face is beet red, glasses still askew. No one is pointing fingers at the mayor's son.

"Kat and Zach lit a piece of paper on fire," I hear someone say.

And before Zach or I can even begin to protest, Mr. Ruth turns to me and Zach and angrily says words I never thought I'd hear in my high school career: "Detention! For both of you!"

2

Mystic Hollow Community Page

NEW POST FROM ABE HENDERSON: I'd just like to say Necco Wafers were a huge hit in my day. But don't worry, trick-or-treaters. My grandkids told me to buy Sour Patch Kids this year.

"I cannot believe this. I should not be in here," Zach says for the tenth time this afternoon. "I did nothing wrong!"

The constant *tap, tap, tap* of Zach's pencil against the desk should make me wince. But all I can think about is how Colton Croft looked at me. And *winked* at me. *Scared you good, didn't I?* Does that mean he put on the Horseman costume . . . for me? Maybe he didn't even want to partner with Zara. Maybe he was just being polite. After all, I saw him open her card and chuck it into the trash, and when Laney and I checked it afterward, it was a thank-you note from her mom to his dad.

Who cares if my spell backfired and I almost burned

down the chemistry lab. No one was hurt, and I finally got Colton Croft to notice me.

"Hadley, what are you smiling about? This is serious and all your fault," Zach grumbles.

"It was your Bunsen burner," I argue. "Your responsibility."

"This is why we should have worked *together.* As lab partners."

"Both of you, quiet," says Ms. Gagliano, who is grading papers at the front of the room while she serves as our detention monitor. Usually, the teachers rotate who proctors detention, but when Ms. Gagliano heard it was the two of us this afternoon, she burst out laughing and said, "This I've got to see to believe." I don't think she's ever forgiven us for beating her at the teacher-student spelling bee in ninth grade. She really wanted that Spirited Books gift card.

Neither Zach nor I have ever stepped out of line in school before. We both hand in our papers early. We do all the extra-credit assignments. We volunteer for every fundraiser, pancake breakfast, and tutoring drop-in center the school runs. We aren't late for classes. We never miss school. Why, I wouldn't be surprised if we both get the perfect attendance record at high school graduation next year.

But it's his own fault for meddling with me. He's always meddling—asking me what I'm doing so he can copy me or poke holes in my logic. It's bad enough that I have to compete with the ghost of a perfect older sister who is off at college. I didn't realize I'd have to compete with Zach Powell too.

"I want to speak to Principal Aceste," Zach says, not quieting down.

"So do I," I chime in. Zach's stare is molten. "What? I'm allowed to talk to him too. This whole thing was an accident." *A magical accident*, I don't add.

"Principal Aceste has to talk to the fire chief and the insurance examiner and calm down Mr. Ruth," Ms. Gagliano says as she circles the top of someone's paper in a fiery red marker and gives them a 75. Oof. "Tomorrow morning, I'm sure you'll both get a chance to meet with him." She smiles wickedly. "I bet he will even call your parents."

My stomach plummets. I didn't even think about that part. If Principal Aceste talks to my parents, my party is done for. Which means spending Samhain—the real name of Halloween—with Colton is also done for. I can't let that happen. My spell would have worked perfectly if Zach hadn't grabbed my hand, I'm sure of it. I glare at him. His mouth is set in a thin line.

He smells like smoke—we both do. There is still some foam in his hair from the fire extinguisher. My own red hair feels a bit sticky from getting caught in the crosshairs as well. "Can't you ask Principal Aceste to meet with us after his calls? I'll wait to explain what happened."

"And what was that?" Zach snaps.

"You wouldn't leave me alone. You shouldn't have gotten

involved, Powell. What I do is none of your business."

"Mr. Ruth made me your lab partner, Hadley."

"Really?" I don't remember an assignment so much as a general suggestion.

Zach rolls his eyes in a perfect circle behind his square glasses. "I know you wanted to work with Colton—"

"And I would've, if you hadn't stopped me."

I hadn't realized we were leaning in toward each other, and I'm uncomfortably putting all my weight into my elbows, until that same tingly feeling creeps up my hands, pins and needles like I've slept on them wrong. I shake them out, flexing fingers to try to get blood flow back.

"I was trying to help, Hadley."

I snort. "Yeah, I bet. Help yourself."

Thankfully, we're both saved by the bell before I can do any more damage.

Ms. Gagliano puts down her red marker and looks at us. "You're free to go, but I'll see you both tomorrow. And the day after that. And the one after that one and . . ." She laughs to herself as we exit the room.

Zach and I take one look at each other and storm off in opposite directions. Laney is waiting for me near our lockers.

"Hey," Laney says sympathetically. "Are you okay? How bad was it?"

I open my locker and start placing every book I own in my backpack. Maybe I'll cram for all my tests next week. I can't leave anything to chance after today. "The room smelled like Lysol and bologna, and we just had to sit there since Zach and I already did our homework during study hall. And I have to go back every day from now to eternity. It's humiliating."

Laney pats my shoulder. "Maybe when you talk to Principal Aceste, he'll listen to you about it being an accident. You two never get in trouble! Like ever."

I sigh deeply and shut my locker. "I hope so." We head to the front doors, and I exhale deeply when we get outside. Leaves are blowing down the sidewalk, the trees on the street in peak form; an array of deep gold, orange, and red leaves greets us, and the sun is just starting to peek behind the clouds. I feel my whole body relax at the sight of Mystic Hollow putting on a fall show.

"Let's talk about something that will make you happy," Laney suggests, hoisting her own backpack higher on her shoulders. "Colton Croft."

"Shhh," I say, looking around to make sure no one heard her. "But yes!" We both laugh and I feel my mood lift. "Did you see how he winked at me? Like *right* at me. I think we had a moment."

"Are you sure? Because he was also having a moment with Zara," Laney reminds me.

"He threw out her note. And he didn't wink at her. I think it's a sign. I've just got to find the right moment to talk to him about my sure-to-be-epic-not-to-be-missed Halloween party, and then it's all going to come together." I frown.

"As long as Principal Aceste doesn't call my parents and the whole thing is canceled."

Laney bites her lip. "No. Don't say that. He hangs out at Witches Brew after school every day. Maybe you can convince him not to call your parents."

"Can I do that?" I think it over. Almost everyone in town goes to Witches Brew after school. Am I going to go beg the principal in front of half of Mystic Hollow High? "Whatever, it doesn't matter how embarrassing it'll be. This party has to happen. The invites are already out. Can you imagine if I have to cancel because I'm grounded?" The idea is too mortifying to think about.

"It's going to be fine. Even if your parents are called, you know they'll never believe you intentionally set fire to the chemistry lab. The party is going to happen as planned. Everyone I've talked to says they can't wait to see your house." She flashes me a little smile. "No one believes me that it's a normal old house, just bigger."

Our Victorian is almost two hundred years old and rumored to be haunted. While witches can see ghosts, they can't in Mystic Hollow. It's part of the wards that we cast every Samhain that protect the town from the other side of the veil.

But maybe for my Halloween party, I can try to conjure one. After all, I lit something on fire today. I could probably do a séance if it would make Colton Croft come to my Halloween party.

For a moment, I let myself imagine it: the perfect Halloween party, where everyone is talking about how cool I am. Me, Kat Hadley. Not Harry. I won't be invisible anymore. They'll see just how charming this witch can be.

"I think the house is a great selling point," Laney says, looping her hands in her backpack straps as we pace down the sidewalk toward the center of town.

"Hey, if it'll get me more RSVPs, I don't care if you tell them we fly broomsticks on Halloween night and resurrect the dead on our dining room table."

Laney's eyes widen. "You've never actually done that, have you?"

"No," I assure her. "I mean, I'm sure there is a spell in my aunts' books, but that sort of zombie stuff totally gives me the ick."

"Good," Laney says, looking relieved. "I know you invited everyone, but I'd rather not attend a party with the undead. Especially if they're oozing into the candy."

We both share a face at that. "I just want this party to be one people never forget," I say, clutching my book bag tighter. "It's my first without Harry home, so it has to be perfect."

This night will change everything. Colton will finally see me, not as Harry's little sister or the less impressive Hadley, but as me. Our eyes will lock and we'll slow dance to "Monster Mash" with my hands around his broad shoulders and his on my waist, and he'll kiss me under a fake spiderweb or whatever the equivalent of Halloween mistletoe is.

"Has Colton RSVP'd yet?" Laney asks. "Halloween is on Saturday."

I shake my head. "It's only Monday. I'm going to remind him. If only we had been lab partners and Powell hadn't blocked me."

"You think he's jealous?"

I snort. "Zach? Yeah, of my grades. You know all he cares about is scoring higher than me. Remember how he was during Word Masters?"

"No, because that was in fourth grade, and I don't memorize every single grade I've ever gotten, because I'm normal."

I shove her with my shoulder. "Okay, well, we'll get Zach out of the way. I'm sure he'll make some excuse about needing to study and won't even come. And with my parents out of town with my grandparents, I just have to get rid of my aunts."

We both inhale deeply as the scent of cider donuts fills the air. We are coming dangerously close to the farmstand now, and neither of us has ever met a cider donut we don't like. "Have you figured out how to get your aunts out of town yet?" she asks.

"Sort of." I fiddle with one of the beaded bracelets on my wrist. "I am going to get up the courage to talk to them tonight. They're supposed to be back this afternoon after some Broadway preview Lin-Manuel invited them to."

"Those two have quite the life," Laney marvels.

My mom's sisters, Vivianne and Diane, live with us part-time in their own wing of the house. The other half of the time, my aunts stay in a luxury apartment near Lincoln Center in New York City that they bought with their latest husbands. Half the time I don't think they even remember that they're married—I never see my uncles. And since neither of my aunts had kids, they spoil Harry and me rotten when they aren't on some lavish trip with their coven.

I adore my aunts, but I do *not* want them chaperoning the party. Those two will not be quiet observers hanging out in their wing. They'll be chatting up the football team, offering to hold séances for the cheerleaders in the library, and commandeering the karaoke machine they bought me for Christmas.

"I just need to tell them that I have a boyfriend. And that I can cast the spells."

Every Halloween our family performs rituals that keep Mystic Hollow's magic alive and protect our small town. All around the world, witch families settle in places with strong magic, where the veil between the natural and supernatural is especially thin. For the Hadleys, that was Mystic Hollow. It makes our magic stronger, but it also attracts more sinister creatures. So, every Halloween, it's our duty to refresh the wards and keep everyone safe. My mom once described it as a symbiotic relationship, but it makes me feel like a little fish suctioned onto a shark, which isn't exactly my vibe.

The Samhain ritual is also the one spell that a witch can't

cast alone. It requires a soulmate—a love so deep that their hearts beat as one. Each partner must share the exact same intention and the exact same sacrifice. Grams used to cast it with Grampa before they moved away to Florida.

Mom and Dad have cast the rituals for as long as I remember, because Dad is the yin to Mom's yang and the spells go perfectly. But this year my grandfather is recovering from surgery, and my parents need to go to St. Augustine. They'll cast the charms in their retirement community to keep them safe. With Harry away, I've been trying to get my parents to let me do the rituals myself this year with my own love match, but I'm not sure Mom actually believes I have a boyfriend. I've been telling the whole family I'm dating someone but don't feel ready to bring him around yet. Sure, it's a bit of a lie, but if things go well with Colton, I will have a boyfriend on Halloween.

"Can you cast the spells? Without a boyfriend?" Laney asks.

"No," I admit as we reach the town green. I kick aside a few extra-crunchy leaves. "But that doesn't matter, because once Colton comes to my party, he'll finally see me, and we'll be in love in time."

"When does the charm need to be cast?" Laney asks, gnawing her lip nervously.

"Midnight. I mean, we usually start prepping the rituals at moonrise—so this year it'll be around nine, I think."

"And your party starts at . . ."

"Six."

"You have three hours to fall in love or the spell protecting our town fails?"

I glare at her. "Haven't you ever heard of love at first sight?" When she opens her mouth, probably to object that Colton has seen me plenty, I add quickly, "And if the spell *works*, then I'll know it's real. That Colton feels the same way about me too. That we're soulmates."

I look over at Laney when I realize she hasn't said anything about this. Instead, she's got a tense look on her face. I feel my fingers tingle as if I can imagine what she's thinking. "You don't think Colton is the one?"

"That's not it," she says carefully. "I just—and don't take this the wrong way—your track record when it comes to finding love on Halloween isn't the best."

"Okay, it hasn't been perfect but . . ."

"Ryan Elliott?" she says by way of explanation. "I remember you threw up three times."

"He wasn't a great pick, but I've evolved."

"Evolved? You still have that wristband in the bottom of your bag."

I feel myself flush. "It was seventh grade."

"Fine, then. Hunter Tyler?"

"Okay, but when we got home my mom was able to salvage that dress with a spell."

Laney's frown deepens, hidden only by a gust of wind

whipping across the green and blowing her hair in front of her face. She opens her mouth, then seems to think better of it and closes it like a fish.

The tingles pulse beneath my skin and I start to sway, feeling ill. "Don't mention Reese Whitaker," I say quietly.

Laney squeezes my hand, a sad smile on her face. She knows how much that one hurts. "I won't," she whispers. "And I'm sorry. I'm being unfair. It's not like I've had better luck!" She rolls her eyes. "I just want someone nice and friendly and smiley. A golden retriever boyfriend. Clearly doesn't exist in Mystic Hollow."

"And I just want someone who sees me for *me*." Not Harry Hadley's loser younger sister. Not a witch who can barely even cast spells. I'm so much more than all that. "But that's going to change at my party." I link my arm with hers. "This Samhain will change *both* our love lives."

"Maybe," Laney agrees as we reach the edge of town.

"Let's manifest it," I decide. So much of magic is about manifesting things. "Anything can happen in Mystic Hollow. This town is literally made of magic."

We both stare at Mystic Hollow's town green, and I have to admit: I get why Mayor Croft is trying to get us trending online for hashtag fall feels or whatever. Our tiny town looks like something from a storybook, the main square set against the backdrop of the mountains in all their fall splendor.

Two dozen shops and eateries in historic buildings are

nestled around the large green space, which looks like a New England college quad with paths crisscrossing it. This time of year, it's filled to the brim with fall decor, scarecrows every few feet, hay bales, and pumpkins. And all the paths lead to a town monument of Harold Croft, who claims to be founder (even though Beatrice Hadley was already here too), and a sign that says "Mystic Hollow, founded 1645." Nearby is our homegrown coffee shop, Witches Brew, which is owned by Zach's family and has the best pumpkin spice lattes on the planet. We also have a Halloween-themed restaurant where I sometimes waitress (and which helpfully agreed to cater my party with a huge employee discount). Along the south side, there's a bed-and-breakfast named All Hallows Inn and stores like Laney's mom's bookshop, Spirited Books, and a candle shop called Coven Candles, plus a hardware store that looks like it was built in the seventeenth century because it probably was. There are ghost tours, leaf-peeping routes, pick-your-own pumpkin patches, haunted corn mazes, a farmstand, and a gigantic cemetery that claims to be where the real Headless Horseman is buried, even though it's just an unmarked obelisk. There is even a parade on Halloween weekend with a Headless Horseman carrying a flaming torch.

But we haven't landed on any fall roundups for Best Halloween Sightseeing because everyone thinks of Salem or Sleepy Hollow first.

Mayor Croft is determined to change that this year. He's

been posting videos that rack up tens, sometimes hundreds of views. (At least fifty of those are me, when Colton is in the videos.)

At the fork in the path, though, I see Colton heading into Witches Brew, and I swerve sharply, nearly crashing into Laney.

"Let's stop in at the bookstore for a bit. Let Witches Brew clear out."

Laney glances over, and I wonder if she can see Colton disappearing into the cozy storefront. A rush of goose bumps travels up my arms, and I fight the urge to wring my hands to shake off the embarrassment.

"I'm not avoiding him," I say quickly, and she startles, like she's surprised I volunteered that info. "It's just . . . I need him to see me at my best. Not when I'm embarrassing."

"Okay," she says slowly. "You know me. I'm never saying no to a trip to our bookstore."

3

Mystic Hollow Community Page

NEW POST FROM MYSTIC HOLLOW FARMS: Extended hours through Halloween weekend. Come get your apple fix with us. Mention your Mystic Hollow address and get a discount!

A tiny bell announces our arrival at Spirited Books. I try to shake the nervous energy out of my hands, but just a deep inhale of that good book smell is enough to put a smile on my face. Fiction, nonfiction, kids, and the supernatural each have their own tiny room in the shop, which was converted from an old home built in the 1800s, like ours. My hands lovingly skim the display of fall-themed books in the front of the shop and the red velvet armchair her mom refurbished. It's the perfect spot to curl up with a book, especially if Laney's cat, Jinx, sits with you.

"Yes, we have a whole section on the supernatural and local history in this room," I hear Laney's mom tell a customer, and the two of us follow the sound of her voice into the next room. "We don't have any books on Mystic Hollow specifically. I mean, there is the guide to town written by Mayor Croft, but he self-published it, so I'm not sure that's what you're looking for."

She's talking to two teens around our age who are wearing coordinating fall outfits and filming the shop on their phones.

Laney and I look at each other. *Influencers.*

Mayor Croft must be thrilled.

"But the town is tied to magic too, right?" one girl asks, holding a ring light in her free hand. "Because we saw a video online that said this is the perfect New England town for leaf-peeping *and* tarot readings."

Laney gives me a look. I stay mum. If this girl considers herself a witch, she isn't the same sort of witch I am. Which is fine, but I doubt she can actually feel the hum of magic here. I mean, it's not like I can either, but the aunts and now Harry are always talking about how much stronger their magic feels when they're here. I've never physically felt my magic, and I'm starting to doubt whether it's inside me anywhere. Although I shouldn't complain—apparently the weight of it can almost be painful. My aunts are always complaining about their knees, and I know my mom's migraines are no joke. Of course Harry would only feel hers in her cute button nose—which is why she sometimes twitches it when she casts a spell.

"Something about ley lines?" the influencer is continuing.

She glances around, like she's about to see a ghost right now at this very moment.

"Stop it!" the other girl says, nudging her. "I don't want to mess with any ghosts or whatever."

"If you don't bother the spirits, they won't bother you," Laney's mom says with a wink, her black bob swaying. She pulls a *Witchcraft of Connecticut* book off one of her shelves and shows it to the girls. "Mystic Hollow isn't even listed in here, which is funny because legend has it this town is a conduit for the supernatural."

Laney gives me a pointed look, like she's saying, *See, those rituals are important and you shouldn't risk all our safety over some guy who I saw picking his nose last week . . . and eating it.*

Or something. It's not like I can read her mind. I shake the tingling out of my fingers. I must be clenching my fists in stress and not realizing it.

"*Great,*" the girl is saying. "We're doomed."

Laney's mom laughs. "No, no. It just means magic is stronger here, so you're right about that. It's an energy. Don't be worried. This town is well protected by a long line of—" Her mom looks up and sees me. "Hi, girls!"

For the millionth time, I wonder if we're as secret about being witches as my mom thinks. We try to never cast out in the open, but I've been called "witch girl" at school for as long as I can remember. After almost four hundred years of protecting the town, I guess we're bound to have started some rumors.

"Hi!" I say, smiling brightly at the girls.

"Hi, Mom. Anything we can help with?" Laney asks. "We've got a few minutes"—I make a noise low in my throat—"An hour," Laney amends.

"Wonderful!" Laney's mom claps her hands together. "Two new fall romance book boxes we've been waiting on just came in, and I haven't had a chance to shelve them yet. Think you could help me out?"

"I'll help too," I say. Something tells me that Colton is going to be at Witches Brew a little while longer.

As I follow Laney to the storage room, a shriek stops me. I whirl to a *thunk*—a book pops off the shelf, followed by another. They land, splayed out across the hardwood.

One girl covers her eyes, but the other holds up her phone, probably live streaming. "Is it a ghost? Is there a presence with us in this bookstore?"

"Nope!" Laney's mom reaches into the stacks and pulls out a large gray tabby cat. "It's just Jinx. There's a crawl space behind some of the stacks, and he finds it funny to make more work for us." She rubs the cat behind the ears, and the cat wriggles to get away.

The phone is lowered with a scowl.

Laney leans over and whispers in my ear, "Next time, she should just say it's witchcraft."

Fifteen minutes later, the shelving is done, and I can't stall anymore. By the time we get to the coffee shop, there is a crowd of people waiting to order and pick up drinks. A group of middle schoolers stands off to the side by the hay bales taking selfies. They each have a tiny pumpkin filled with iced coffee, topped with whipped cream, cinnamon, and fall sprinkles. They laugh as they try to squeeze into the picture with their drinks, and I shake off a pang in my chest. Harry and I took a selfie here, after the fiasco with Ryan at the carnival and I puked up all my cotton candy. She cut the POP wristband off my arm, and I stuffed it in my backpack. It's probably still there, but it reminds me more of her than of him.

I don't remember the last time my sister and I hung out like that and just talked.

"You don't need to get anything," Laney says. "Principal Aceste is right over there." She points to the familiar form in the corner, cheeks hollowing out as he sucks on a huge pumpkin drink.

My nerves are making my fingers tremble. "I could use some caffeine."

Laney gives my shaking hands a knowing look. I'm stalling and she knows it, but Colton and his football buddies are over in the corner, kicking around a pumpkin like a soccer ball. The line should take at least ten minutes. These are complicated drinks.

"Katherine Hadley," a voice calls, and I step forward in confusion to the pickup section. Zach hands me a pumpkin heaped with whipped cream. "Pumpkin spice latte. Extra whip. Extra white chocolate. To go."

He made me my drink? Did Laney text him? "What?"

"It's a long line."

"So?"

"Don't want you getting bored and setting anything else on fire," Zach says, cutting his dark eyes at me. I blink, my stomach lurching as I notice some whip caught in his curls. "What?" he asks, eyes softening.

Before I can stop myself, I reach over with a thumb and brush his hair clean. My cheeks burn. Why did I just do that?

"You should wear a hairnet," I say quickly, trying to sound annoyed.

He only grins back at me, like he's won an argument. "Wait."

That same mitt-sized hand lands on my wrist. I freeze as he knocks a shaker over the cloudlike puff of whipped cream, depositing cinnamon. How did he know I wanted that? Before I can say anything, Zach's brothers are calling him back to manage the line.

When I reach Laney, she's shaking her head.

"What?" I ask. "He just wants me out of his hair."

"His hair," she repeats. "Looks like you were very much *in* his hair."

"That's what I said."

She laughs again. "Whatever. You've both got it bad. I'm just curious who is going to admit their crush first."

"The only crushing I'm doing on Zach Powell involves my GPA totally defeating his. And I'm sure he feels the same."

"Then why didn't you have to pay for your drink?" She leans forward and takes a long sip on the straw. "And why does he know your order?"

I roll my eyes. This is just Zach proving he's better than me. That he has a near-perfect memory and pays attention, unlike me. That he's serious and good at his job.

The one good thing about this terrible conversation is it makes me want to actually embarrass myself by sitting down at a table with our high school principal.

"Katherine," he says, sounding surprised.

"I wanted to, um, apologize for the accident earlier today."

He frowns. "It may have been an accident, but there was extensive damage."

"Extensive?" My stomach rolls. "I'll replace Zara's notebook, and the fire wasn't even that big—"

"The water damage, Katherine. From the sprinklers. I'm going to have to sit down with your parents tomorrow to discuss paying for damages."

"Paying for damages?" My heart hammers in my chest. Despite the sweetness of the pumpkin latte, I think I might throw up.

"I was actually going to give your parents a call right now."

"Don't!" It comes out too urgent, too loud. "Um, my mom just got a new number. Can I give it to you?"

I glance over at Laney. Can I have him call her instead? She shakes her head, mouthing, "Don't even think about it." Who else, then?

Barking breaks through the lull of the café, and a dog comes barreling through the cozy space. Principal Aceste flinches, his drink spilling spectacularly all over the floor, as Zach steps out from behind the counter just in time. The pup jumps up and places his paws on Zach's stomach, barking happily, and Zach actually smiles.

I've seen this dog before. He's brown with a patch of black fur running along his back like a skunk, and he's not wearing a collar.

"Ronald! There you are!" Zach rubs the dog on his head.

"Fred!" Laney runs over now too, and the dog turns to her and tries to lick her face. "Good to see you, buddy!"

"Fred? It's Ronald," Zach tells Laney.

"No, I call him Fred. He looks like a Fred," Laney insists, and the two start arguing.

I bend over to help clean up the principal's spilled drink. His phone has also fallen. My heart jumps into my throat.

"Whose dog is this?" Principal Aceste asks, his voice sharp.

"He's a stray," Zach says. "I've been trying to gain his

trust for days. I left food out for him last night, but when I got too close, he ran off."

"We did too, but we couldn't get him into the shop," Laney says, and starts cooing to the dog again. "Want a treat? Do you, boy?"

Zach pulls a dog bone out of his pocket. "Here you go, Ronald. It's pumpkin!"

The dog sniffs the bone then grabs it and runs off. Of course Zach carries dog treats with him.

"It is a health violation to have dogs in here," the principal is saying. I share a look with Laney, flashing his phone.

"Are you sure that's true?" she asks, distracting the principal as I paw around in his phone. "Because I know Mayor Croft has reworked the town charter this Halloween season—"

Zach is glaring at me. He sidles closer, dropping his voice and his lips so they're right by my ear. "What are you doing, Hadley?"

I scroll through his contacts to my mother's number. Of course they've been texting about my sister, Harry, and how wonderful she is.

I go to change the number to Laney's, but my fingers buzz and fumble across the screen. To my horror, a few numbers seem to magically change.

"Then I'll talk to the mayor myself," Principal Aceste is saying. As he stands, Zach and I wrestle for the phone.

"You dropped this," Zach says, holding it out.

"Ah, thank you," Principal Aceste says, glancing between the two of us. "Very kind of you."

As he walks away, Zach yanks a hairnet over his curls. "You'd better be fixing this, Hadley."

4

Mystic Hollow Community Page

NEW POST FROM ANONYMOUS: Stray dog seen wandering around Mystic Hollow. Brown. Looks like a retriever mix. Friendly, but easily spooked. Anyone know who the owner is?

I button my coat and keep my head down as I hurry home, wondering what will happen when Principal Aceste tries to call my mother and gets a stranger instead.

Maybe I can cast a spell that the stranger will play along, pay for the damages, and this will all be resolved without my parents finding out, so the party won't be canceled, and Colton Croft will prove his love to me magically at midnight on Halloween?

Yeah, right. Even Harry isn't that good of a witch.

She'll probably laugh about it with my mom. It's so embarrassing that my spell backfired so epically. The thought of Harry hearing about this makes my whole body tingle like a rash. I can feel a pit forming in my stomach.

As dusk starts to settle over the mountain behind our town, the sunset seems to highlight our house at the end of the street. For almost two hundred years, it's been perched on the edge of the lake, the gables framed against our weeping willow.

The garden grabs me—it's gotten unwieldy since Harry moved away to Boston for school—but I like the messy look of the ferns and trailing ivy. Even the large oak tree in the center of our lawn seems to have grown wilder without her. I feel that same pinch in my chest—the tire swing is starting to fray. If we don't do anything, it'll fall into the yard soon. I convinced Harry to cast a spell that would get the tire to swing without us pumping our legs, and the two of us would spend hours outside, taking turns, laughing, and talking.

Lately, we haven't been doing either of those things. We used to work together so well. Harry was good at everything, and I was good at, well, Harry. I knew how to get her to loosen up, to take a break, to do something a little bit against the rules.

And while our parents would discipline us and tell us to get back to work, Dad would always give me a little smile. "You're good for her Kitty Kat," Dad told me once, patting me on the back.

That was the one thing that I could do. I couldn't cast spells or win awards, and even my straight A's weren't worth a comment, since Harry was every teacher's favorite. But I was good for her. *We* were good.

But it doesn't feel that way anymore, and I don't know why. One minute Harry had my back, and the next she shut me out completely. Ever since then, we've been like ships crossing in the night. Pleasant to one another, but every conversation we have is surface level. I feel like I've fallen behind and I can never catch up. She'll always be two years older, and I'll always be just following in her footsteps down a path she already carved.

My phone beeps. My mom is asking why I'm still outside—she can sense where we are, I think, and she's antsy for our weekly video call with Harry. It's the worst part of my week. My parents and aunts basically spend an hour gushing over Harry and Boston College.

My parents are professors, and it's like they've unlocked some secret language now that my sister is at college. My mom compares my sister's syllabi to the one she has for her class Witches and Witchcraft in the Early Modern World. My dad gives her advice for talking to professors during office hours and complains about the TAs for his Folklore and the Fantastic class. And they both spend at least ten minutes extolling my sister's magic and spell work, even though my dad isn't a witch and doesn't have any magical blood.

All while I sit there with nothing to add.

And yeah, I know I sound jealous. Maybe I am. I just want someone to see me, and I've spent my entire life feeling invisible. With Harry three hours away in Boston, this year was my chance to stand out on my own. And now with one spell gone wrong, I might have gone and blown up everything.

Because chances are Principal Aceste has my dad's number somewhere, and once he can't get through to my mom, he's going to call him. And then I'll be grounded for the rest of my life.

Even walking as slowly as possible, I still reach the wraparound porch. Small white candles flicker in the windows, giving the house a glow as I run up the steps, being careful to sidestep the one loose board. I pause at the door, until it creaks open on its own—or, more likely, thanks to Mom's intention.

I'm greeted by the smell of leaves and sage intermixed with apple and have to imagine Mom is smudging the house and Dad is making an apple pie, which he does every week in the fall. Steeling myself with a deep breath, I follow the harmony of their low voices to the kitchen. The floor creaks as I walk across oriental rugs scattered here and there for warmth.

Our home has always felt a bit like an antique shop. No two pieces of furniture seem to go together, and yet somehow the place works. There are the hurricane lamps from a trip to Salem last Thanksgiving, the leather armchair my parents got on an anniversary trip to Portland, and the deep blue velvet couch from their St. Augustine trip to Grampa and Grams's for a solstice celebration. The fireplace crackles away, staying lit even when no one is there to restock the wood, and the ticking of the grandfather clock passed down from generations past steadies my racing heart. From her croissant shape on the sofa, our cat, Phoebe, taps her fluffy gray tail, yellow eyes following me through the room like Great-Aunt Aida's portrait.

"Kitty Kat? Is that you?" Dad calls.

"Of course it's Kat," I hear Mom tell him as I walk tentatively into the kitchen. "She's been loitering in the garden for some reason."

So she definitely felt my presence. I try to arrange my face somewhere near neutral as I step into the kitchen. My parents flank the massive oak table built by my great-great-grandparents that anchors the whole room. Bright, shiny white subway tile surrounds cabinets, some open, revealing apothecary jars next to things like peanut butter. A pendant light hangs over the island, providing lots of light, but it's the little lamps on most counters and shelves that give all the warmth. Well, the lamps and my dad, who beams at me like I just hung the moon.

Next to my mother's glower, it almost feels sarcastic.

"Kitty Kat!" he says. When he pulls me in for a hug, he smells like cinnamon; the gesture surfaces a cloud from the flour dusted on his sweater, one of a dozen of the Halloween-themed ones he's bought over the years. He is trying hard to make Ugly Halloween sweaters become a thing like Ugly

Christmas sweaters are. It hasn't happened yet. When he pulls back, he looks at me as if seeing me for the first time, his brown eyes warm, his short reddish hair, so similar to mine, smelling like grapes thanks to some homemade pomade he's been working on forever. "How was your day?"

I pause, feeling my body go taut as a bowstring as I look from Dad to Mom. "Good," I say cautiously, bracing for impact. "How was yours? Talk to anyone?" *Any calls?*

"No. Just your aunts. I've been busy getting ready for this trip."

I silently cheer. Maybe I can cast a spell without them seeing and fix this whole thing.

"We've just been packing," Mom says. "It's taking forever, though. I've had a migraine all day. But that always happens this close to Samhain."

She lets down her slick blond bun, just as smooth and Barbie-doll perfect as Harry's hair, and massages her temples. "How about you? Any . . . symptoms?" Mom and Dad stare at me, waiting for an answer about magic. I might have a cough from setting the chem lab on fire. Does that count?

"Why are you favoring your left hand?" my mom pushes, reaching out.

I glance down, unsure. "Oh, I got a paper cut while reshelving books with Laney. It's nothing."

She inspects the minuscule red line. "Does it hurt? That could be a symptom. I've never heard of a Hadley needing to bleed, but feeling your magic in your fingers could be possible—"

"It's a paper cut," I say, a little sharper than intended. "Just a paper cut."

It hurts how disappointed they both are.

"Would you like a Band-Aid?" my dad offers. "I'll get you a Band-Aid."

I sigh. As my mother looks around, probably trying not to let her crushing disappointment play across her face, I reach for the glass jar of candy corn and candy pumpkins we leave on the counter all fall. By the end of October, there are only candy corn left. I have a thing for the candy pumpkins. I know they're the exact same candy and, sure, they taste like wax, but I love them. I start fishing out a pumpkin. My fingers close around two at the same time. "Don't worry. Peter and I have gone over the rituals, and we're ready for Samhain. I'm going to nail the ritual this year, I promise."

Peter. As in Parker. My imaginary boyfriend. I've never been so happy that my parents hate comics.

"We can't wait to meet Peter," Dad says, hustling back into the room with an entire first-aid kit. "Do you think he'll be free before we leave for Grams and Grampa's?"

"I don't know," I mumble. "He's got that big science project due. It's about . . . spiders. He's big into science. Which is why he's the perfect person to help me with the Samhain rituals."

Mom's lips purse. The woman is a human lie detector, but this time she doesn't say anything. "I still feel so guilty leaving you to deal with this on Samhain. I know you have your aunts to help you, but this is a big responsibility." She wrings the kitchen towel in her hands. "You need to have a real . . . connection." She seems to struggle to find the right word, which is a rarity for the brainiac witch professor that she is. She looks to my dad for help.

He, too, seems a bit unsure. "What your mother is trying to say is we don't want you feeling pressured to do this. Your aunts are happy to give their husbands a call."

I'm not sure they remember their numbers, but I'm not saying that.

"Dad's right, though." Mom drains a bowl of pasta into a colander in the kitchen island sink, and steam fills the air, fogging her face. "If you and Peter don't feel ready, Aunt Viv and Aunt Diane can manage. The rituals need to be done by people with a strong bond, and they've been married for, um, well, I think it's been at least a year. A decade?"

"These ones, it was . . . did they have a fall wedding?" my dad asks.

"What we mean to say is you and Peter have only been dating a few months, right? It's early. No shame in having the aunts step in—"

"I'm ready," I insist, even if I do need to finalize things with my supposed other half. "I'm not going to let you down.

Haven't I proven myself around the house? Taking out the trash? Trimming the herbs in the greenhouse? I even sang to the Venus flytrap the other day to get it to eat every insect and it listened."

Mom brightens. "Really? Victor usually only opens up when Harry sings to him."

I ignore the Harry mention. "Well, Victor and I are besties now. I sang 'Monster Mash' to him and he loved it." I squeeze Mom's hand. "I am not going to let you down. I know the protection spells by heart, and I'll follow them exactly that night." And this I truly mean. "The last thing I want to do is mess up the veil between Mystic Hollow and the supernatural world."

Mom smiles, her shoulders relaxing. A pot of homemade marinara sauce stirs itself with a large wooden spoon on the stove while she shakes out the pasta noodles. "It's just such an important night. I feel bad we'll be with Grampa and Grams."

"Nic, our daughter's got it," Dad says, placing a comforting hand on my right shoulder. "This girl was prepared coming out of the womb. Remember that time I knocked over a candle during our dance lesson in the dining room? This girl was the first one to get to the fire extinguisher."

I can tell my mom isn't impressed, though. Because I didn't use magic.

Just another reason I can't let her find out about this morning.

Dad beams at me. "Kitty Kat always gets things done." He looks at me proudly. "You don't have to worry about her protecting Mystic Hollow."

My heart warms. "Of course I will! The Halloween party is not going to get in the way of that." I open the candy jar again and reach for another pumpkin.

Mom's wooden spoon flies over and swats my wrist. "Kat, we're about to eat!"

"I have room," I mumble. "And that hurt."

"Sorry. But the party, is that still happening?" Mom asks as the napkins next to her leap into her hand. She hands them to me to put on the table. "I haven't heard you mention it in a while."

I feel a twinge of panic that she's suddenly questioning this. "Because everything is already set and I know the rules. We'll stay on the first floor. I'll keep people out of the greenhouse and have the whole house cleaned up before midnight."

Mom's eyes widen. "Midnight?"

"I meant ten thirty," I say hastily, feeling the waxy pumpkin get caught in my teeth. "Which leaves plenty of time to do the rituals at the house right before midnight. Laney will help me prep long before moonrise."

Mom purses her lips and I fear she's going to say something I will not want to hear, but then her face lights up. "Oh! That's your sister! She's about to call!" She stands the iPad up against the pasta bowl. I guess we're having cold pasta tonight. Because Harry has to call right now. "Everyone, gather round. I think she's just getting back to her dorm room in three . . . two . . ."

I know better than to question my mom's premonition skills. Dad and I cram in, and I try to relax. Principal Aceste hasn't called. Harry is away at school. My Halloween plan is still very much on track. But all my fears come roaring back as the video call connects and Harry's perfect face lights up the screen.

5

Mystic Hollow Community Page

NEW POST FROM RITA BAUMANN: Witches Brew appreciation post! I'm so thankful I live in a town that would never allow a chain coffee shop. Witches Brew makes the best lattes in New England, and these new theme drinks that come in gourds are genius! Especially since they buy the pumpkins from our very own Mystic Hollow patch!

The call connects on my sister, Harriet Samantha Hadley, curled up on her dorm room bed. Even dressed in gym clothes, she looks like a model. Her long, blond hair practically glows, it's so shiny. Her green eyes blink twice as she adjusts her phone to get an even better angle of her face.

As she tilts the camera, we get a snippet of her background: sage-green bedding, an artful smattering of pillows in pinks and creams. It looks like someone's Pinterest come to life. Could she at least forget to make her bed once? Fall prints are framed on the wall beside her bed along with a few family and friend photos tacked carefully to a corkboard.

"Harry!" Dad says happily. "I was just telling the mailman the story of your acceptance. He couldn't believe that you got advanced standing. My BC girl!"

Harry smiles, her voice quiet. "Dad, you shouldn't keep him from his route." Her soft voice grates on me from hundreds of miles away.

"He's just run out of people to brag to," Mom gushes. "You look wonderful. By the way, do you have a copy of that essay you wrote in eighth grade on the politics of witch trials? I want to use it as an example for my college seminar . . ." My two parents crush into frame, squeezing me out so they can get their eldest daughter's attention. It's like I don't even exist. Somehow, they find new achievements to congratulate my sister on. This week, they're praising her for sending them a few news articles and primary sources that were "absolutely perfect" for their curricula.

"My genius girl finding the time to text her silly dad," my dad is saying.

I hid a scoff with another candy pumpkin. *Who cares that you never call or text me? Who cares that we haven't spoken since the last video chat? Why should it bother me that you act like I don't exist?*

"You aren't silly, Dad." Harry winds just one perfect strand of blond hair around her finger and then abruptly sneezes.

"Harry? Is your magic manifesting?" my mom asks excitedly. She taps her temple. "I don't feel anything—"

Harry's eyes shift along her phone screen, and with a jolt I realize she must be looking at me. "You look different."

"Me?" I squeak out. Is that supposed to be a compliment or a knock? "Um, thanks? I think?"

"Yeah," Harry continues, squinting. "How was your day? Anything special happen?"

Oh, you know, I conjured a fireball, almost burned down the chemistry lab, stalked my principal, and hacked into his phone. "Nope. I did get a paper cut." I hold up my finger as evidence.

"I've been meaning to ask—do you have your chemistry study guides at home?" Mom interrupts. "They were so thorough and I was thinking they could be helpful to Kat."

"Mom," I gripe.

Harry rubs her nose and then frowns. "Something tells me that Kat has been totally *on fire* in chemistry."

My parents whip to stare at me as I fight the urge to glare at Harry. She looks back innocently, perfect brows raised.

Don't you dare, I think at her as hard as I can.

And then Harry twitches her nose.

Suddenly there is a video beeping in from a number I don't recognize. My stomach drops. Principal Aceste! Did Harry just make him call? She's literally the worst. Thankfully, Mom ignores the request. Nothing to interrupt her perfect Harry time. That is, until the call lights up the screen again. Mom tries to dismiss it, but before her finger brushes the screen, I hear her gasp.

"Oh, it's your aunts! I've been trying to get them all day," Mom says, accepting the request. "Viv? Diane? Is that you?"

All we see is one giant blinking eyeball, rimmed with kohl liner and gold eye shadow and layers of mascara.

"Is it on?" Aunt Vivianne's voice blares out, with a rush of music and laughter from the background. "I don't see anyone."

"How should I know?" comes Aunt Diane's voice. "Didn't you ask Hugh how this works?"

"I don't even know if he remembers handing me the phone, dear. I just said, Jackman, you wolverine! Hand it over! And he did."

"Aunt Viv," I say, jumping in now. "Hold the phone away from you and look at the screen. You'll be able to see us."

"Oh, Kat!" Half of Aunt Viv appears. Her blond hair is cut into a short, stylish bob, and I can see one long, dangling gold earring. Aunt Diane—with her shoulder-length sandy-brown hair, deep-set brown eyes, and youthful face—crams in next to her so that we can see half of her face too. "There you all are!"

"I've been trying to reach you all day," my mom says with a sigh. The youngest of three charmed ones, my mom was born years after Viv and Diane, but sometimes it feels as if my mom is their parent. "Why aren't you answering your phones?"

"Phones?" Aunt Diane says. She turns to Aunt Viv. "Do we have those?"

My mom massages the bridge of her nose. This is definitely a non-magical headache. "I wanted to ask if your husbands are in town. We might need them for Samhain."

"Husbands?" Aunt Diane asks.

Aunt Viv snorts. "We definitely don't have those."

"Except—" Aunt Diane interrupts.

"Oh, right. We may have left them in Triora—"

"Glastonbury—"

"I distinctly recall seeing at least one of them in Hólmavík—"

Both aunts nod. "We can acquire husbands before Samhain, dear," Aunt Viv says. "If ours are still . . . um . . ."

"Lost," Aunt Diane corrects.

"Missing," Aunt Viv agrees. "Is that all? We'd like to get back to the party, and while we always love a little tête-à-tête, we're still planning to return, oh . . . tomorrow evening?"

"Not tomorrow," Aunt Diane whispers. "Sutton Foster mentioned brunch."

"Oh yes! That's right," Aunt Viv said. "Can't we discuss all this in two days' time?"

My mom kneads her scalp. "Halloween is this Saturday! With Mommy being unable to travel this year, I want to make sure our Samhain plan is set in stone."

Every year, Hadleys around the world cast protection spells in their neighborhoods, since we've all settled places where magic is strongest. Mystic Hollow has always been supercharged, so Mom and Dad take it as a priority, but this year, Grampa had hip replacement surgery and he's still not up and running, and it was agreed Mom and Dad would go there, so Grampa and Grams's community wouldn't be in danger. I volunteered to stay here to perform the rituals with . . . Peter. And my mom agreed, only because she is demanding my aunts come into town with their husbands as a backup. Or at least, that was my mom's plan. I just have . . . another plan.

"I still feel uncomfortable leaving town on the most important day of the year," Mom is saying to the group. "I haven't missed a Samhain in Mystic Hollow in over thirty years."

"Oh, Nic, relax!" Aunt Diane says tartly. "Mystic Hollow has survived for hundreds of years. It's not about to fall now because another Hadley has to perform the spells. We're blood."

"Should you be talking about this at a party?" Mom asks my aunt.

"Oh please," says Aunt Diane, waving her hand and showing off a diamond tennis bracelet. "No one can hear us. Hugh's penthouse is packed with people and—oh look!—there's Jenna Bush Hager. I love her. Hi, Jenna!" she shouts at the top of her lungs. "Viv! We have to go say hi—"

"Diane!" Mom pinches the bridge of her nose. "Focus. Me first. Then Jenna."

"Fine," Diane says like a child, and I can't help myself. I glance over at Harry on the screen to see if she's smiling like I am. Whenever the aunts were being, well, the aunts, we'd always make eye contact and fight the giggles.

I'm not sure if I imagine it, but I feel like Harry's eyes flicker across her screen like she's looking at me too.

But Harry looks down at her perfect manicure so fast, and it feels a bit like the sun disappearing behind the clouds again. What did I do wrong?

"I love you all, but I have some studying to do," Harry says briskly. "I'm gonna go, okay?"

Dad puts his arm around my mom. "It's all right, my love. All will be well." He looks at me. "Kat and Peter will take care of everything, and your sisters are here if she needs help."

"Peter? Who is Peter?" Harry asks, and my stomach drops.

"My boyfriend," I say, keeping my tone light. I grab an apple from the fruit bowl in front of me and squeeze it like a stress ball.

"You have a boyfriend? Since when?" Harry demands. She's squinching her nose up and down like a bunny rabbit.

"Since . . . all fall. Since you left," I insist, feeling my brow prickle with sweat.

Harry's eyes narrow. "Peter who? I don't know any Peters."

"You wouldn't. He just moved here," I say. "I mean, he moved over the summer, but we met when school started and . . ." I take a deep breath and try to get it together. "The point is Peter is my boyfriend, and Mom and Dad said we could do the protection spells. We've got this covered, Harry. You go enjoy BC."

"But—" Harry goes to interrupt.

Suddenly the broom leaning against the wall slams to the floor, startling everyone. The screen door outside the kitchen starts to flap back and forth, slamming, as if the wind picked up.

Mom looks at the door curiously. "I should lock the greenhouse. Dear? Can you set the table for me?" Mom asks Dad.

"Of course, my love," Dad says, grabbing plates and moving to the dining room.

"Any other Broadway stars there?" I ask the aunts, to try to keep them talking so it's not just me and Harry alone on a call. But the aunts trade a look.

"Hugh's getting a call," Aunt Viv says.

"We definitely shouldn't answer it," Aunt Diane adds.

The two look at each other, cackle, and then their video chat abruptly disappears, which leaves me alone with Harry on the call that no one seemed to officially end. Despite claiming to have urgent studying to do, Harry doesn't hang up.

"Kat, who is Peter?" she asks calmly.

"Harry? Why do you even care?" I sidestep. "Just go

enjoy yourself in Boston." I can feel my stomach tighten, my emotions getting the better of me.

Harry glares at me. "You're lying to Mom and Dad. I know you don't have a boyfriend. You can't."

"Why, because who would want to date me?" I ask sarcastically, but my voice catches so it comes out strangled, whiny.

"I know you don't have a boyfriend," she says again, and her voice is so even I want to throw my mom's phone into the wall. "I know you want one every Halloween, but this time there's more on the line. You can't risk all of Mystic Hollow because, what, you have a crush?"

I feel a scream building my throat.

"Have you even asked him to do the rituals?" Harry presses, twitching her button nose. "Have you spoken to him . . . at all?"

I reach forward to end the call before she magically stumbles into any other truths when she says, "Does this one even know your name?"

This one. The screen goes black and I see my own face reflected back to me. I look like a gargoyle. *This one.* Because I have no shortage of boys who broke my heart.

Boys of Halloween Past

CRUSH #1: RYAN ELLIOTT
THE YEAR: SEVENTH GRADE

"Please, please, please, please, PLEE-ZE?" I beg my sister, standing behind her in our bathroom giving her zero personal space. "It will take two seconds!"

"Kat! You'll never learn how to do spells if I always do it for you." Her eyes are on the mirror, where she is applying her third coat of mascara. Harry has always been great at mascara.

"But you're just so good at it!" I take a strand of her gloriously soft blond hair and hold it between my thumb and index finger. "I remember what your hair was like when we were kids. And this summer it's suddenly frizz-free? You fixed this with magic."

Harry drops the mascara wand, and it bounces into the sink as she spins around to look at me, smelling like a mix of mint leaves and vanilla, a scent she made herself because it was her boyfriend Chris Branton's favorite. (Chris stats: high school freshman and founder of his very own after-school initiative: Save the Patch, a group dedicated to promoting local pumpkin patches in New England. There has never been such a town outcry as the year Mayor Croft found out some people were buying their Cinderella gourds from Trader Joe's.)

"No, I didn't," she insists, but I can see her cheeks reddening.

"You did," I sing. "And I know you used mom's favorite silk shirt!"

Harry slaps her hand over my mouth to keep me from talking, but I am relentless, like all seventh graders are.

"She's been asking where it went for *weeks*, and I'm going to tell her you burned it, all to get silky hair. You're gonna be in so much trouble!"

My sister and I share everything. A pale gray cashmere zip-up sweater the aunts gave us, shoes, and even exam notes. We binge the same shows, listen to the same music, and half the time I talk about something, I can't remember if the idea is mine or Harry's. She is my sister and my best friend. (Laney is very okay with being a close second because Harry frequently gets her books early, totally not through magical spells.)

The only thing we don't share is magic. While Harry has mastered hers, I'm not sure I even have any.

Harry's left eye begins to twitch, which is a sign that I am getting to her. She adjusts her forest-green crewneck sweater she's paired with jeans. I may have been teasing her for being vain, but this is the first Halloween that she barely looks dressed up—her only festive Halloween touch is the tiny Headless Horseman earrings we both got at one of Mystic Hollow's Saturday farmers' markets. Meanwhile, I've gone full Halloween, like any witch should. But don't worry—I made it cute! My Spirited Bookstore tee is adorable and fits nicely under our coveted cashmere sweater. It could be witchcraft, but my new jeans definitely make me look taller. And, best of all, my braces came off this afternoon. My makeup is decent. My scent is Bath and Body sponsored, and my breath is minty fresh. All I need now is good hair. Hair that Ryan Elliott can't ignore.

He'll take one look at me and realize that we aren't just friends. We have to be boyfriend/girlfriend.

I've been telling Harry for weeks he's been flirting with me. "Morning, Sunshine," he says every time he walks into English and sits down next to me. "You smell good," he said yesterday, getting a whiff of my vanilla body spray. I used the rest of the bottle tonight—Harry isn't going to be thrilled when she gets this sweater back, but it's totally worth it. And when we started talking about the Halloween carnival, I told him that I'd never been on any of the spinny rides, even though the entire seventh grade can't shut up about the Gravitron ride. Apparently, the bottom drops out, and Tom Callabra did a backflip when he was pinned to the wall by the centripetal motion. I even told him how, last year, I waited in line with Harry six times and chickened out each time. That's when Ryan said, and I quote: "Let's go be brave together."

Together. Tonight is the night.

Or it will be, once I have good hair.

Harry takes my brush out of my hand, and I watch as she plucks a strand of my red hair. Rolling her eyes, she ties a knot in it, then again, and again. I watch, open-mouthed in glee—when Harry does magic, it really does feel magical—as she whips out a lighter and my scraggly red hair goes up in smoke. Immediately, my hair goes from rat's-nest curls to the cutest beach waves ever. I gasp as the bathroom door opens and Mom walks in.

"Everything okay?" she asks. "It smells like burning hair in here."

"Sorry," I chirp, and throw my arm around Harry, making a show of unplugging the curling iron. "Look how amazing Harry made my hair look!"

"You both look great," Mom says, smiling happily. "Have fun at the carnival, but remember to be back before eleven to be here when Dad and I—"

"Do the Samhain spells," we say in unison.

"We know, Mom," Harry replies for both of us. "We wouldn't miss it."

I have plenty of time. When I come back tonight, I'll have my first boyfriend.

"Are you sure you don't want us to wait with you to find him?" Harry asks.

Chris has his arm around my sister, his JV Headless

Horseman jersey on even though we don't have any games on Halloween. I've never seen him without it, and lately I haven't seen Harry much without him.

"Ryan will be here any minute," I assure her. "He already texted saying he was on his way. Go. Have fun. I'll meet you back here at this exact spot at ten thirty."

Usually, I have to be home much earlier, but this is Halloween. The Hadley version of the Super Bowl. One of the most important calendar days of the year, according to my mom and the aunts. Curfews go out the window. Besides, Harry is nearby. My parents aren't worried.

"Okay," Harry says, pursing her lips slightly and smudging her rose-colored lip gloss. "Be careful."

"Okay, Mom!" I wave them off, then look around the carnival, which smells like a funnel cake and cotton candy had a baby. The place, as always, is packed. The carnival is in the parking lot next to Mystic Hollow High, like it is every year. Kids from the middle and high school mill around eating treats, playing carnival games with Halloween-themed prizes, and riding the rides, which is what I cannot wait to do. I look around the sea of heads, hoping to spot a boy with dark brown hair. I am certain he'll be wearing a hoodie with a flannel unbuttoned over it and joggers. I am not sure Ryan owns a pair of jeans. That's okay. We all have our flaws.

"Kat!"

I hear him before I see him waving to me, trying to get past a long crowd waiting to go on the Ferris wheel. Then he's jogging toward me, his brown eyes and long lashes are brighter in the glow of the carnival lights.

"Hey," I say, trying not to sound nervous, even though my heart is beating so hard, I wouldn't be surprised if he could see it through my tee and sweater.

"Hey." He sounds out of breath. "Sorry I'm late. Practice went long and I had to go home and shower."

He showered for me! Well, for all of Mystic Hollow, really. "It's okay. I haven't been waiting long." My fingers tingle with excitement. "So should we get our POP wristbands and hit the Gravitron first? We can be brave together."

He laughs. "Anything you want, Sunshine."

The two of us approach the ticket booth to buy the Pay-One-Price wristbands. A wristband, I am sure, I will cut off and hang on my wall for all of eternity. Then someday I'll tell our grandkids, "Your grandfather and I had our first date at the Halloween carnival in seventh grade . . ." and I'll ramble on till they roll their eyes like I do at my grandmother sometimes.

"Next!"

We step up to the counter. "One POP, please," I say, my hand on my bag to retrieve my wallet. I don't expect him to pay for mine.

"That will be thirty-four dollars," the girl behind the glass window says. I accept my wristband with a surge of excitement and turn to look at Ryan. For some reason, his face falls.

"Oh, crap."

"What's wrong?"

"I forgot my wallet at home." His big, beautiful eyes crinkle with worry. "I'm sorry, Sunshine. I think I'm going to have to take a pass on rides tonight."

My heart feels like it fell out of my chest. No! This is not how tonight is supposed to go. We go on the Gravitron together, then tackle the mirror maze, ride the coaster, and then have our first kiss on the Ferris wheel. I have it all mapped out. We have to go on rides!

I open my wallet and look inside. The babysitting money I've collected from the Murphys over the past month stares back at me. There is just enough for a second POP and some food later. "What if I bought it for you?"

"Wait. Seriously?" When he puts a hand on my arm, my stomach back flips. "You don't mind? I'll pay you back. Better yet, I'll pay for yours next year when we come together."

It's official. I've stopped breathing.

"It's a plan," I say, and hand over the money. Soon, Ryan is rocking a matching wristband, and we're off toward the far corner of the parking lot turned Halloween fair. He walks close, his shoulder bumping mine the entire way to the ride, and I have to remind myself to speak when I am supposed to answer a question. But inside, I'm all butterflies, walking around with him, nearly touching. It's finally happening.

I'm not even nervous when we get into line for the spinning ride. Not if we're together.

Then his phone pings. "Shoot!" Ryan looks at me apologetically. "It's my mom. My younger sister hasn't checked in. Can you hold my spot? I'll be right back, I promise. I'll meet you on the ride. Just stay here, okay?"

"Of course," I say, because how cute is it that he is checking on his younger sister? I could swoon. "It's a long line. I'm sure you'll meet me before I even get to the front." The Gravitron ride line is always the worst. Why we all wait so long to be spun at warp speed is beyond me.

"You really are the best, Sunshine," he says, hugging me again. As his arms brush my back, I feel like I might die. "See you in a bit." And with another smile and wave, Ryan disappears into the crowd.

My phone pings too.

Laney:

How's it going?

Me:

Amazing!

I fill Laney in on everything as the line inches forward. By the time we stop texting, I'm nearing the front of the line and there is still no Ryan.

Didn't he say he'd meet me on the ride? I crane my neck,

looking for his mop of brown hair.

"You can go ahead," I say to the couple behind me.

"No," says the high schooler running the ride. "I remember you. Either ride or get out of line."

"C'mon," says the guy behind me, and next thing I know I'm being shoved onto the ride.

The door shuts with a resounding *clang*, and I feel like I might have a heart attack.

Then we start spinning. The world pulls around me. Everyone is laughing and screaming, and I clench myself tight, counting the seconds until it's over.

When I wobble my way down the stairs back to the pavement, I'm half expecting Ryan to be there. To be proud of how brave I am.

But he's nowhere to be found. He must be trying to find his sister, but the carnival isn't that big. He'll be back soon, and he won't want to wait long to ride with me.

I get back in line.

The second time is worse. I feel like an egg being scrambled.

But the third really takes the cake.

When I get off after, it feels like the entire world has transformed into a spinning carnival ride. I can barely read the numbers on my phone screen, but there's no denying that Ryan hasn't texted me and it's been over an hour. I am debating what to do when the crowd seems to part, and I see him playing the carnival ring-toss game. Is he trying to win me a giant plush Frankenstein as an apology? That would be so cute—except when he wins, he hands the stuffed animal off to Ali Meadows. She squeals and throws her arms around him. He whispers something in her ear, then the two turn and head for the Ferris wheel. Together. When he puts his arm over her shoulders, his POP wristband catches the light.

My POP wristband. The one I bought for him.

He was never going to go on any rides with me. He just wanted to save thirty-four bucks.

The realization sends me to the nearest garbage can. As the world finally crashes back to stillness, I puke my guts out.

A hand manifests in my hair, gently holding it back, another on my back, rubbing it softly. "Breathe," comes a gentle voice.

Harry. When I whimper and stand, she wipes at my mouth with a napkin and offers me a ginger ale. I don't ask how she knows what happened. It doesn't matter how she knows; I'm just relieved that she knows, that my sister is here, and while everything is awful, if she's here, she'll make it better.

"What do I do now?" I ask as the tears start to fall.

"We're going home." She hands me a tissue, smoothly accepting the soda back.

"We? It's only nine o'clock. You and Chris still have—"

"Chris will understand," Harry says, putting a gentle arm around me, leading me away from the flashing lights and the happy screams of the carnival goers. "Sisters come first."

We never utter Ryan's name. But on Monday morning in class, when he sits down next to me, his chair somehow shatters, breaking into a million pieces and sending him hurtling to the floor. When I get home, Harry is sitting at the kitchen table on a plastic folding chair from the basement. I don't ask what happened to her chair, but she has a splinter in her thumb, and the woodpile on the porch is twice as tall.

6

Mystic Hollow Community Page

NEW POST FROM MAYOR CROFT: This is your mayor again. A gentle reminder, people, that shaving cream and toilet-papering the mayoral home will not be tolerated this Halloween. I promise you, fellow Mystic Hollow residents, I will find the Toilet Paper Bandit of 2025!

Just after seventh period, the intercom crackles.

"Katherine Hadley to the principal's office," comes Mr. Aceste's voice, and that's when the panic hits me. I try to focus on breathing deep as I walk down the halls, shaking the nervous energy out of my hands, but it doesn't help when I hear one of the secretaries talking about the thousands of dollars of damage caused by the sprinklers. I stop at my locker to pick up the brownies I baked last night—Laney and I brainstormed and decided it was my last chance to butter him up, literally.

When I get to the office, Mr. Aceste's secretary is on the

phone. I had been hoping for her sympathy, since she always secretly lets me call my mom if I've forgotten my laptop charger, but she won't even look at me. Okay, so I'm doomed. Principal Aceste's door is closed, and I can't imagine sitting in one of the chairs he keeps by his office, so I wander around instead. The photocopy machine is whirring at a hundred beats a minute in the adjacent room, and just outside the windows the hallways are packed with students going to the last period. I've been sweating all day waiting for this meeting. In third period, Zach wouldn't even look at me, but just kept pushing his glasses higher and higher on his nose so I think he was nervous too. I'm not sure when he's getting called down, but he's not here. Maybe he talked to Principal Aceste at Witches Brew after I left. Maybe he's off the hook.

Then I hear yelling in the principal's office. Everyone in the office stops what they're doing and trades worried looks. I can actively feel my armpits dampen. Principal Aceste is not a yeller, so this has to be bad. The next thing I know, the door flies open and Zach comes striding out, his face pale.

Crap.

"Send her in," Principal Aceste calls in a strangled voice. "Now!"

"Go ahead, dear," his secretary says, not looking up from her desk.

Perhaps "doomed" was optimistic. I glance after Zach, but he's already halfway down the hallway, so what can I do but take a deep breath and walk into the principal's office to face the music? Principal Aceste is facing the window so I can only see the back of his head. The office walls are filled with Red Sox memorabilia. On his desk sits a waterlogged chemistry textbook. It's leaking a river down toward his keyboard.

I wince. "Good afternoon, Principal Aceste. I made your favorite. Peanut butter brownies." I place them on his desk, my nerves making my hands shake.

He spins around in his chair, and suddenly my stomach explodes with hunger. In fact, I'm suddenly really tempted to grab one of the brownies that I made just for him.

"Thanks, Kat." He pulls one of the brownies out and eats it immediately, and suddenly the ravenous beast of my stomach goes quiet. I pat my belly. That was weird. Then he checks his watch.

"I'm certain I told them to be here at two."

I freeze. So, he did call them. Even though I stayed up late last night baking, my parents didn't talk to me about it at all. Did they not get the call? They would have said something to me. I'm sure of it. "They're on their way," I lie. "But that's good because I was hoping to talk to you alone first. I really want to apologize."

"Me too," he says. "I'm sorry if you just heard yelling. Zach and I just got into it about last night's World Series game." His gray eyes blink as he stares at me, and I slowly breathe out. Of course. Zach is definitely a Yankees guy. "But we did also talk about the damage." He prods the slushy pages on his desk. "I have a meeting after school with the

PTO about funds. What am I going to tell them?"

"That it was all an accident?" I say hopefully, balling my hands at my sides. "Principal Aceste, you know me. I would never cause a fire in school. I love this place! I want to be valedictorian next year. Please, just tell me what I can do to make things right." I push the brownie tray closer to him. Maybe he's just hangry. But it's not like I could feel his hunger earlier—Harry can't even do that. My mom, maybe, but I'm not my mother. "This really was a mistake." I draw in a slow breath. "My mistake. Not Zach's."

"And what exactly happened?" Principal Aceste asks as he helps himself to another brownie. "I was speaking with Mr. Powell, and he told me that the Bunsen burner malfunctioned, but we just bought those last year. And when I pressed him about it, he just kept saying he didn't know. I need an answer, and I need to know if our lab equipment is unsafe."

I gape at him. Zach lied for me? I know he saw me burn that piece of paper. But that's not what he said. I don't know what to do. My chest tightens and I cross my arms to hide how my hands are shaking. I open my mouth, hoping the right words will come out, just as I hear a commotion in the hallway, big voices and laughter. The door to Principal Aceste's office opens, bringing with it the scent of grapefruit, licorice, and hints of amber.

Aunt Vivianne and Aunt Diane blow into the room like a beautiful storm off the sea, chattering away, arms laden with multiple bags. Aunt Vivianne, always the more serious of the two, is dressed in a fitted pantsuit and black heels, while Aunt Diane looks like a fairy sprite, her hair pinned off her face with a fresh pink rose that looks just like the ones on her dress, and she is wearing glittery cowboy boots.

What are they doing here?

"You must be Principal Aceste?" Aunt Vivianne is shaking his hand effusively. "I know you said two, but my sister and I were regrettably delayed coming from our charity work."

Principal Aceste blinks in shock. "Yes, you must be . . . Diane?"

"Vivianne," she corrects. "So unfortunate that Katherine's parents were busy teaching, but it's a good thing you got through to us instead. After all, it would be a crime to pull such talented professors away from their students. Such a noble profession, don't you agree?" Her voice is crisp and polite.

But they don't have classes on Tuesday afternoons, I think, and my aunt turns to me, as if she's heard my thoughts. She gives an almost imperceptible wink.

The tension deflates from my body so quickly, I'm surprised it doesn't make a rude balloon noise.

"Of course," Principal Aceste agrees, looking stunned.

"I see you and Kat are already talking. About the accident, I presume. As it was an accident. My niece would never set fire to anything! The very thought of our straight-A darling girl doing such a thing is preposterous." She sits right down and crosses her legs. "Isn't that right, Diane?" She flattens her lips and looks back toward the hall. "Diane?"

Aunt Diane lingers in the doorway, her attention on the secretary in the other room.

"I just wash my face with good old-fashioned soap, Renee," Aunt Diane says. "But I'll send you the name of the loofah I swear by. Oh! Principal Aceste!" She crosses the room and shakes his hand vigorously. "How are you?"

"Oh," he says, looking dazed. "To be honest, I have been a bit stressed."

"Completely understandable!" Diane tells him, batting her thick lashes his way. "A man as powerful as you, in charge of the school and all these students. Don't worry. I've got a wonderful cream that helps with stress. A bit on the temples and—voilà!—your headaches will be gone." She pulls a tube of unidentifiable cream out of her leather handbag and dabs it on his finger. He amazingly does what he's told and rubs it into his brow line.

And I can almost feel my shoulders relax, as my head stops throbbing.

Wait. When did my head *start* throbbing? I shake the weirdness off.

"Wow, that is amazing," Principal Aceste is saying. "I can almost feel the stress melting away."

"It is," Diane insists, and pats his hand before returning to our side of the desk and squeezing my hand. "I'll drop off a larger tube. It's made with rose petal leaves and—"

"Diane, I was just telling Principal Aceste our dear Katherine would never set fire to anything," Aunt Vivianne interrupts. "It was faulty equipment. Nothing more. I am sure of it. Why, it could have hurt a student. But no worries. I don't even see that much damage, do you?"

"No damage?" Principal Aceste's eyes widen, and he extends a hand to gesture at the book. "We're talking about a thousand gallons of . . . oh." I follow his gaze down to the pristine hardback. He rubs his temples again. "How is that possible?"

"Miracles do happen," Aunt Diane says solemnly. "Such good luck that the small fire our niece witnessed didn't trip the sprinklers at all. And, well, now we just have the matter of the faulty equipment that needs replacing."

Aunt Vivianne waves a check in front of Principal Aceste's face. "This generous donation from an anonymous patron of the arts should cover whatever you need." She waits before handing it to him. "Now that we both agree that the lab equipment was entirely at fault. Not our dear niece."

"And not my lab partner either," I say hurriedly. It's the least I can do after he gave me that PSL yesterday at Witches Brew. I don't need him thinking that I owe him or anything.

Principal Aceste takes the check, and his eyes widen. "This is too much."

"Nonsense." Aunt Vivianne waves her wrist loosely, and it sparkles with her gold bracelets. "It's for the children, after all." She stands and so does Aunt Diane. "So I take it we're finished here?"

"I . . ." Principal Aceste looks from one of my aunts to the other and grins. "Yes. Of course. The PTO will be thrilled to hear it." He's practically giddy now. "Kat, please let Zach know I won't be calling his parents. Detention is canceled. Just please be more careful next time. And remind Zach that Yankees attire isn't permitted on school grounds."

"Of course." I feel a rush of warmth in my chest and resist leaping over the table and hugging Principal Aceste. Who I really should be thanking are my aunts. "Thank you so much!" I can't wait to text Zach.

I love telling him, *I told you so.*

"Thank you, Principal Aceste," says Aunt Diane, looping her arm through mine. This close, the sweetness of licorice fills my nostrils. "We are going to take Katherine with us. The poor girl has been so stressed, I don't think she's eaten a thing since yesterday."

"You won't be marking her absent for eighth period, now, will you?" Aunt Vivianne adds as she stands and loops her leather carryall bag through her arm. Both my aunts stare at the man expectantly.

"No. Of course not." Principal Aceste's cheeks redden. "Have fun."

7

Mystic Hollow Community Page

NEW POST FROM MYSTIC HOLLOW PTO:
Apparently reports of the chemistry lab being destroyed were exaggerated. The lab is fine! And thanks to an anonymous donation, the science department has money to buy brand-new lab equipment.

"Tell the truth," I say as my aunts breeze out of the high school with me in tow for a late lunch. "How did you know about my meeting?"

Aunt Vivianne and Aunt Diane smile at each other mischievously.

"Like you don't know," Aunt Viv says, and her eyes glitter.

"I really don't," I say with a nervous laugh.

"Because unless your principal is secretly best friends with Wolverine, it's pretty lucky that he happened to call the phone we were holding, looking for your mom."

My heart stops. I remember the aunts hanging up on

our call because their borrowed phone was ringing. I also remember typing the wrong number into Principal Aceste's phone because my hands were shaking. The spilled drink. It's not exactly the perfect sacrifice, but if my intention was strong enough . . . could I have cast a spell?

"Lucky, or maybe magical?" Aunt Diane says, with another wink. "Of course, you can always call us to swoop in and save the day. It's what we're here for."

"Thankyouthankyouthankyou!" I gush, bear-hugging them on the school steps.

"But we do want to hear all about it," Aunt Diane says as she walks quickly to her car that is parked illegally in front of the school. "And you can tell us over lunch."

"Okay," I agree, my chest ballooning with hope. Once I tell them that I successfully cast a spell, they'll definitely agree to leave me unchaperoned on Samhain. "If I can ask you who wrote that check you gave Principal Aceste."

"Ummm . . . let me think," Aunt Vivianne says as she starts the car. "Diane, who did we tell we needed money for equipment at the high school? Kristin? Or was it Leslie?"

"Oh, I don't remember. Everyone wanted to help when they heard the school burned down," says Aunt Diane, getting into the passenger seat.

"But the school didn't burn down," I remind her.

"Technicality," says Aunt Vivianne, flooring it. We race through the school zone, the speed pressing me into my seat. My aunts just don't have to worry about speeding tickets.

"The money went to the school, didn't it? And they wanted to remain anonymous, so all's well that ends well."

I'm a bit skeptical, but I'm instantly swayed when I see the clear bag filled with candy pumpkins Aunt Diane is passing me from the front seat. "We got these for you in the city, dear. From some sugar factory to celebrate."

"Celebrate?" I ask, taking the bag and opening it up. I smell a hint of vanilla and caramel. I pop a pumpkin in my mouth and decide to save the rest for Zach as a peace offering. He's been texting nonstop after my "We're all clear! Detention canceled!" text. I haven't had a chance to write him back. With detention off the table, all that's left to do is convince my aunts they don't need to be home.

"Your talents, of course," says Aunt Viv, taking a sharp right turn into town that sends me tumbling into the adjacent leather seat. "Getting a phone call to manifest is one thing, but we're so proud that you blew up the chemistry lab!"

"I thought you told Principal Aceste it was an accident," I say, and pause. "Plus, 'blew up' is a bit of an exaggeration."

She turns to look at me, crossing her arms. The wheel continues to twitch on its own as the car zooms down the tree-lined streets, orange and red leaves blurring. "That, my dear, is your magic at work."

I might as well accept it. "Right," I say. "I was just, you know, practicing. Honing. Since I'm doing the rituals this year alone with . . . Peter."

"Peter!" says Aunt Diane, clasping her hands together.

She looks teary as Aunt Viv—or whatever enchantment has the car—pulls neatly into an open parking spot on the town green. "Look at how you've grown this year. I know you've been so worried that your magic wasn't as strong as ours, what with no ailment to let you know it's working, but clearly you were wrong. You started a fire! That's some serious spell work. The rites will be a cinch compared to that."

"About that," I say, nerves prickling along me. "Since I'm clearly coming into my powers so well, I was wondering—well, hoping—that you two might consider letting me do the ritual on my own."

"On your own?" Aunt Viv asks, and her tawny hazels are suddenly serious.

I gulp. "I mean, you were just saying how proud you were—"

"That's a tall order, little miss," Aunt Viv says, trading a look with Aunt Diane. "For you, and for . . ."

"Peter," I say, a moment too late.

Aunt Viv finds my eyes in the rearview. "Right. *Peter.*"

"If only we could meet him," Aunt Diane says. She rubs at her knee—that's where she generally feels her magic. Which is the last thing I need.

A knock on the car window makes me jump, but the aunts only smile. I turn to see Zach, as the aunts sweep out of their seats. Zach opens the door for me, his brow furrowed.

"Kat? Are you okay? Why haven't you been texting me back?" Zach asks, gently shutting the car door behind me.

Aunt Diane smiles like the Cheshire cat. "We were just talking about you."

No, we weren't.

Wait. My aunts think that Zach is "Peter"?

"You definitely are the perfect partner for our Kat," Aunt Viv says before I can deny it. "I can feel the chemistry!"

Zach smiles, scuffing a hand through his curls. "Thank you. That's what I've been trying to tell her."

I bite my lip, curling fingers into fists to hide the nervous tingles. While it's gross to think of Zach as my boyfriend, as long as he thinks we're talking *lab* partners, I just might be able to pull this off.

"Speaking of, um, chemistry," I say, reaching for Zach's elbow. Somehow he reaches for me at the same time and our hands meet instead, and the aunts all but *aww* aloud. When I take his hand, I feel a shock rip through my hand, like static after taking a sweater out of the dryer. My body tingles seem to ripple like waves. If Zach notices he doesn't say, but his cheeks do go a little pink. I only grip his hand harder. Who cares. I'll hold hands with Zach Powell if it means I can convince the aunts to leave me—and Colton—alone together. "We do need to talk. Maybe, um, alone." I turn to my aunts, who are all starry-eyed. "Can you two get a table? We'll be right in."

"Take your time!" Aunt Diane says with a grin as I pull Zach a ways down the block, hiding us behind a giant cornstalk display in front of Mystic Hollow Bakery. His hand is warm against mine, and maybe I'm not in a hurry to let go. At least this way he can't escape and tell my aunts the truth. The scent of butter and fresh bread is in the air. In the window are beautifully iced tiny witch hats, ghosts, and pumpkins. In the distance, a line wends its way out of Witches Brew and a carnival ride truck goes whirling by, headed for the school parking lot.

"Where are we going, Hadley?" Zach asks, squeezing my hand. I ignore the rush of warmth. "I've got to get to work."

"What are you doing skipping eighth period?" I ask.

"I had a dentist appointment," he says. "What are you doing?"

"I just got out of my meeting," I admit. "Like I texted. Everything is fine. The chem lab is actually . . . fine." I try to sound chipper.

Zach's right eyebrow shoots up behind the chunky black frame of his glasses. "Fine?"

"Yep. All fine. Plus, my aunts got this generous science donation so Principal Aceste is happy, and Mr. Ruth will be happy, and detention is over so we're back to our regularly scheduled bickering. I even brought you a peace offering. Candy corn?" I hold up the bag, not expecting him to take one. No one likes candy corn but me. I once read it's in the top five of least liked Halloween candies.

"Oh wow, you got the pumpkins too," Zach says, opening the bag. "Sweet! These are my favorite."

I'm sort of mad. I had been expecting him to reject my

gracious gift—then I'd get to eat all of them. "So, truce?" I ask. We're already holding hands, so I offer my other hand to shake.

Zach glances down at it, lips twitching up in a smile. "Truce."

Now we're standing under the green's largest sycamore tree. Fall has burnished it gold. And I'm clasping both hands with Zach Powell, like some sort of handfasting ritual.

I quickly let go. "Cool. Thanks. See you in chem, I guess." I turn to go meet my aunts.

"Oh, before I forget," he says, and I swivel back. "My brothers and I are coming to your party. Does this count as an official RSVP?"

"A text would have been nice," I say, and he gives me a look. "See you tomorrow, Powell."

"See you tomorrow, Hadley," he says, and for some reason, my eyes are glued to his back as he walks across the green. It takes me a moment to snap out of it, and I wander back down the street to the bistro. My aunts are perched in a front window table, slurping on tea with their pinkie fingers out.

"We saw that," Aunt Diane says like a song, looking smug as she stares at me over her reading glasses. "The energy between you two . . . it's divine."

"Electric is what it is," Aunt Viv. "You and Peter are a wonderful match."

"Yes, well, thanks," I say, feeling my cheeks redden as I sit down and pull my menu in front of me. My aunt takes it out of my hands and puts a book in its place. It's brown leather, the size of a journal. I stare at the gold lettering. *A Guide to Your Magic*. The subtitle: *You're Changing and Your Magic Is Too!* I blink hard. It feels like one of the health class manuals they handed out in fifth grade when they wanted us to learn about good hygiene and our ever-changing bodies. Both of my aunts stare at me expectantly. "Ummm . . . thanks?" I thumb through it and stare at the short spells with names like "Curse Me Nots," "How to Hex Someone,'" and something called "Finding Your Spiritual Pet." Whatever that is. While a spell only requires an object to sacrifice and intention to manifest, generations of witches have found particularly powerful combinations—a doll to represent a loved one; particular words that help guide the magic.

I've studied spell books before, but never one that felt like it was made specifically for a teenage girl.

"Now that your magic has come in, these are some spells that might come in handy," Aunt Diane explains.

"We know you're tentative, dear, but look how far you've come," Aunt Viv says encouragingly.

My fingers shake with fear, and I let the book close. *I haven't mastered my magic*, I want to confess. But if I do that, they won't leave town on Samhain. *It will be fine, Kat. You've seen the Samhain rituals a dozen times. Don't fall apart now.* So instead I say, "You're right. I have. Which is why you and Uncle Jeff and Uncle Owen should go on that cruise you've been eyeing. I found the cruise pamphlet." *Only because I'm the one who planted it in your rooms.*

"Uncle who?" Aunt Viv starts to say, then shakes her head. "Oh, them! How'd you know about the six-month cruise?"

"You told me about it," I lie. "You said it sounded amazing."

"It does! But I'm sure it's sold out by now."

"Why don't you check?" I ask, my heart hammering. I can feel it beating in my fingertips. As the aunts bend into their phones, bickering about how to open the web browser, I scrounge in my backpack. A stick of gum, a lip gloss, Laney's bookmark, the broken POP bracelet from seventh grade.

That's sort of a ticket, isn't it?

Quick as I can, I submerge the paper in my water glass, dunking it beside the ice. The paper prunes, wrinkles, and dissolves. A sacrifice. I close my eyes tight and whisper, "Please get them a ticket."

"Oh! Look at that! Two cabins. It's fate!" Aunt Diane trumpets.

I snap eyes open at the swirling water glass—all clear. The POP bracelet is gone. Did I just cast another spell?

"Buy it! Quick!" Aunt Diane says.

Aunt Viv pauses, finger poised over the screen. "But if we go, you'll be all alone for Samhain. He seems like a lovely boy, but I'm not sure it's wise to leave you and Peter here alone."

"Though I guess we could use a portal if we had to get back quickly," Aunt Viv murmurs. "Or you could call Harry."

Not that I ever would. I try to keep my face neutral.

"Oh, that's true," Aunt Viv says happily. "Your sister isn't far. She could get here to help you."

I clutch the new magic book to my chest. "You don't need to worry. I can do this with Peter. I don't need Harry." I stare directly at Aunt Viv, who has picked up on my divide with Harry more than anyone in the family. "I've got Samhain under control. And if something comes up, I'll call you. I promise."

Aunt Viv purses her lips and thinks for a moment. "Okay," she finally says. "This Samhain is all yours."

Inside, I'm screaming. I can't wait to tell Laney! The house is mine for Halloween! We can finally start getting ready. I stare out the window across the green at the navy-blue Victorian, which is the Croft house. It's all happening. This is going to be the best Samhain ever.

8

Mystic Hollow Community Page

NEW POST FROM MAYOR CROFT: Halloween is just three days away! You know the drill, people. No street parking this weekend. Buy extra candy. Keep your porch lights on for trick-or-treaters. Put your best holiday foot forward. We want our tourists to see that a trip to Mystic Hollow in the fall is one they'll want to take every year—especially for Halloween.

When I wake up Wednesday morning, it feels like Christmas. I can hear Dad and Mom talking quietly and the sound of luggage thunking down the stairs. The old pipes in the house creak when someone is showering, and I can picture my aunts in their wing of the house rushing to get ready to leave for their flight to Miami to catch their cruise (whether Uncle Jeff and Uncle Owen are going, who knows). I still can't believe I cast a spell to get them tickets. In a strange coincidence, Mom and Dad's flight to Florida leaves around the same time so they're sharing a car service.

Which means that in less than an hour, I'll have the entire house to myself.

I pick up my cell phone, turn off Do Not Disturb, and click on the evite I sent. There's quite a few new RSVPs. Tom Callabra has invited three people, I see, without asking me. Grrr. I couldn't get out of inviting him. He practically hunted me down in the halls, he's so excited to see our "haunted house." Still no RSVP from Colton, though.

I text Laney: House will be ours tonight! Can you come over after school and help me make a list of things we need to tackle before the party?

Even though it's seven a.m., Laney replies right away, like the best friend she is.

Laney:

Ummmm . . . yes!

Me:

Great! I need your help storing some Hadley heirlooms I'd rather people not see.

Laney:

Yeah, that picture of your great-aunt Aida always freaks me out. It's like her eyes are following me.

Me:

They are.

Laney:

Wait. Seriously?

Me:

I mean we've always thought so, but my aunts have never confirmed it. Apparently, she was always on my aunts and mom about honing their magic and not wasting time on frivolous things like boys.

Laney:

Gee, now I can see why she never married.

Me:

I'm also thinking we want to hide my mom's ceremonial daggers and lock up the greenhouse.

Laney:

Yeah, the last thing you need is for Victor to bite someone's hand.

Me:

He's a Venus flytrap. He eats flies.

Laney:

I'm telling you, he bit me when I sang Mariah Carey to him. He's clearly not a fan.

Me:

Who doesn't like Mariah???

Also . . .

Colton hasn't RSVP'd yet. Should I text him separately? Or is that too much?

Laney:

Send one more group text. Say you need a head count for . . . punch.

Me:

Punch? Is this Great-Aunt Aida from the grave?

Laney:

LOL. Burgers?

Me:

Yes! See you soon!

I shoot off a large group text: Three days till Halloween! If you're coming to the party and want to eat, get back to me today—I'm ordering from Haunted House of Hamburgers for all the ghouls and ghosts on my RSVP list.

I can't decide if "ghouls and ghosts" is cheesy or festive.

"Kat?" my mom calls from downstairs. Everyone must be getting ready to leave. I hit Send and jump out of bed in my Halloween pajamas Aunt Diane bought me (a pattern of tiny little witch hats and broomsticks cover my tee and pj pants). Before I even reach the door, my phone buzzes. Someone is up and replying already! I rush back to see the message and my phone nearly slips from my hands.

Colton Croft:

Ohmygodohmygodohmygodohmygodohmygodohmygod!

Colton is coming to my party! I fight the urge to let out an ear-piercing scream. I'll hold it till after the adults leave and share my news with Great-Aunt Aida instead. Quickly, I text Laney a screenshot. She screams over text with me. A thumbs-up! From Colton!

Another text comes in too, and it's from Zach: Hadley, what do you need for the party? My mom says you like her apple spice cookies and she'll make some for me to bring. Is that okay?

I grin to myself. If I had to lose some of the candy pumpkins, at least I'm getting something better back. Zach's competitive nature is almost useful. I should've started this sweets war a long time ago.

I text back: Sure! and hear my mom yell again and the sound of a car horn outside. "Coming!" I drop my phone, do a small kick of my heels in the air, and practically float down the hall like the spirits people think roam this house.

Everyone is waiting for me at the bottom of the stairs. Mom has the family spell book in her hands. It's big and the color of an eggplant, with cream-colored pages that are crinkled and sometimes stained from various spell work. Without even opening it, I know the spells in this book are ancient, passed down from generation to generation of Hadleys till one thought to compile them all in a book several hundred years ago. The spells are handwritten, in various handwriting and fonts, with suggestions for the right objects and words to use. And they aren't quite as fun as the hairdo enchantments that were in the book my aunts gave me. This one has spells that curse unfaithful lovers and bring back the dead and even the ones used to protect Mystic Hollow. My hands tremble as I reach for the book, which smells like ash and leather, but Mom only grips it tighter.

"Are you sure you're ready?" Mom asks one last time.

"Nic, for the love of warlocks, hand the kid the book," Aunt Viv admonishes. She's wearing a headscarf and big black sunglasses like she's about to take a ride in a convertible. "She says she can handle this. Believe her." My aunt gives me a tiny nod.

"I know, I know, but this is so much to do on your own, and if this Peter doesn't help you like you say he will—"

"Then she'll call Harry," Aunt Diane says. "Right?"

I can't bring myself to lie to my aunts. "He'll help me. Because our love is true." *Or it will be, once I tell him how I feel. Because he has to feel the same way too.*

Mom nods, but I can tell she's still uncertain.

"Kitty Kat wouldn't tell us she's ready if she wasn't, my love," Dad chimes in, placing a hand around the small of my mom's back. "She's got her necklace. She is well protected."

I touch the purple amethyst around my neck. Harry and I have identical necklaces. They were a gift from the aunts when we were young. The crystals were cut from the same stone, meant to link the two of us and offer family protection—I can only guess at what the aunts sacrificed to imbue these with such a powerful protection spell. Aunt Viv said no matter how far apart we are, the energy in the stone will always connect us. Lately that distance has been more mental than physical.

"And if she's confused or has questions, she can call us." Dad looks at me and I nod effusively. "We do have cell service in St. Augustine."

"Oh, and we haven't given Kat our special gift for her first Samhain ritual on her own!" says Aunt Diane, who is also wearing oversize sunglasses along with a beach hat. She leaves her floral luggage and runs into the living room and returns with a giant hatbox. "For you, my dear. We ordered it weeks ago, but it just flew in this morning."

"Flew?" I take the hatbox.

“Boring details,” Aunt Viv answers for my aunt, flapping her hand to dismiss the question. “Open it so we can go. And then, Nic, give that child the book already. She’s ready. We all are. The plane isn’t going to wait for us.”

I open the hatbox and peer at the black hat nestled inside. My dad starts to chuckle. My aunts grin. I let the box fall away as I pull the hat out. It’s a traditional witch hat, the kind you see in stories and movies, the ones where witches are sometimes green and fly around on brooms. This one has a glittery black ribbon around the base of the hat, circled by a wide brim. These hats are more folklore than necessity, but Aunt Viv, my mom, and Aunt Diane started wearing them on Samhain as kids, and the tradition has been carried on every year since—when a witch comes of age and is ready to participate in Samhain, she gets a hat. Harry had one by ninth grade.

For some reason, the sight of this hat makes me nervous. This is actually a big deal. The protection spells. The need to have a true love casting them with me. I worry for a split second that I’ve bit off more than I can chew, but then I remind myself: Colton Croft gave me a thumbs-up. I can do this.

The car honks again.

“All right. That’s enough. Put the hat on, Kat,” Aunt Viv instructs. I do like I’m told, fitting the hat over my bed head. It fits tight, the tip of the hat bending ever so slightly. With the biggest smile, Dad takes out his phone and snaps a picture that Aunt Diane immediately requests because she can't find the camera on her own phone. And then Aunt Viv is yelling again, kissing me on the cheek and leaving with Aunt Diane right behind her. Dad gives me a big hug too, and then it's just Mom, me, and the book.

I hold my hands out again. If she notices how they're shaking, she says nothing. This time Mom relinquishes the book. It's surprisingly heavy and almost warm, heating my hands. Before I can say anything, she wraps me and the book in her arms for a tight hug. "Trust yourself and your magic," she whispers.

"I will," I tell her, and then because I'm suddenly feeling emotional about the whole thing, I say something else I've been bottling up all week: "It really means a lot to me that you are letting me do this."

Mom pulls back and looks at me. There's something in her expression I can't read. My fingers tingle, and I get the overwhelming sense that my mom has something to say. "You two are going to do great," she whispers.

And then I'm waving goodbye in the doorway, forgetting the witch hat is still on my head. I watch the car roll away, then slam the door and am greeted with the sound of silence.

Surprise and elation war in me. And then I feel the biggest grin stretching across my face. I did it! I really did it! Halloween alone—and with Colton Croft.

"Alexa!" I yell as I put the spell book safely on the hall table. "Play Halloween music!"

"Werewolves of London" fills the air, and I dance around the center hall in front of Great-Aunt Aida's portrait, so elated I could scream. My fingers are tingling, my hips are twitching, and I'm scream-singing so loud that the chandelier rattles. I have the whole house to myself. I can shake my butt and sing as much as I want!

"Nice moves."

I turn around and my heart turns to stone in my chest. "Harry?"

My sister is standing in the doorway in a quilted vest and jeans; a large duffel over her right arm and a roller bag next to her.

"Don't look at me like that," Harry snaps. "I'm not thrilled to be here either."

Boys of Halloween Past

CRUSH #2: HUNTER TYLER
THE YEAR: EIGHTH GRADE

"Let's get on the dance floor! I want to see your best ghoulish moves!"

The bleachers clear and eighth graders hugging the walls of the muggy gym migrate onto the gym floor, under flashing orange and purple black lights as the Yeah Yeah Yeahs' "Heads Will Roll" begins to play. I am standing by the punch: small gummy eyeballs floating in a green concoction that tastes like liquid sugar. Next to me, Tom Callabra is slurping directly from the bowl like an overgrown dog.

"What are you looking at, witch?" he says with an overly loud, annoying laugh as he walks away, his Headless Horseman football jacket slung over one shoulder.

"This is one of those times when I really wish you knew your spells and could strike him down with a massive acne attack right here on the dance floor." Laney is next to me, her eyes like slits as she watches Tom drift away.

"Me too," I say with a sigh as I sip a watered-down

lemonade. It's the Nightmare Before Halloween Howl for eighth graders. I begged Harry to serve as one of the high school volunteers, and she even got her boyfriend Kevin to DJ. She's over by his booth, giving Band-Aids to one of the girls from the swim team.

Our eyes lock and I offer her a little smile. It's so nice knowing my older sister is here looking out for me. Plus, she's so cool. I'm so proud to be the great Harry Hadley's little sister.

Plus, I look pretty cute myself, even though my gothic belted black dress has a tulle skirt that is basically made of itches. Laney has gone for a dress that has a black top and a white skirt splattered with blood that a few teachers frowned upon. I think it looks perfectly Laney, who is nervous and chattering a mile a minute.

"We should get out there and dance, right?" she asks me, her tiny red earrings swaying.

"My sister said people don't couple off until the slow songs," I tell her, feeling proud to show off my older sister's knowledge. "And she said it'll be at least halfway through the dance before Kevin throws in anything slow."

"I can't believe you're going to slow dance with a boy tonight," Laney gushes. "Have you seen Hunter yet? I mean, have you seen *the woodsman*?" she corrects herself, using the assigned code word for my crush, Hunter Tyler.

He has big green eyes, freckles that run across his nose

and cheeks, a gap-toothed grin, brown hair, and favors the Model UN over organized sports. Instead of dirty sneakers and sandals with socks, Hunter always looks like he's heading to an internship. He even wears dress shoes to school. Finally, I've found a smart boy who cares more about his grades than toilet-papering the mayoral mansion! We are perfect for each other. There is only one tiny issue: I hear he has a thing for Zara Patel.

Insignificant details.

He hasn't asked her out, and he hasn't asked her to dance either. I have been watching his side of the gym all night, and Hunter has never left the bleachers, where he is sitting with his friends. Meanwhile, Zara is in the center of the gym floor, wearing a skintight orange dress that has tiny black cats all over the skirt.

That's when a sweeping orchestral chord echoes through the gymnasium. I glance over and Harry is giving me a thumbs-up, as "I Put a Spell on You" has all my classmates coupling off and swaying.

This is my moment. I have to seize it.

"We aren't halfway through!" I say in a panic. My hands start to itch—they've been feeling weird whenever I'm nervous or stressed.

"Now's your chance!" Laney says, gently pushing me toward Hunter.

"But he's with his friends! I need to find a way to get

him alone to ask. I am not walking up to him in front of everyone."

"Good plan," Laney agrees. "Should we pull the fire alarm?"

"Noooooo! That will end the dance! Fire Chief Upton will never let us back in here." I tap my foot trying to think of another idea. And that's when my fingers start to tingle and the hair on the back of my neck stands up. I listen to the lyrics, and inspiration strikes. "I will do a spell to get him to notice me."

Laney's eyes brighten in the glow of the disco ball flashing on the dance floor. "Yes! A spell. You know one to use? I mean, can you actually do it?"

"Yes," I decide, clutching the crystal necklace my aunts gave me for strength. I think hard about one of the intention spells I read about in my spell book. "I'm going to write Hunter's name down on a piece of paper and burn it in a cauldron."

Laney frowns. "So you're going home? Or did you bring a cauldron in your bag?"

"I didn't bring a cauldron! Though a pocket-size cauldron could be a good invention. I'll use a sink. I just need paper and matches, and the bathroom all to myself, so I can say my intention and light the paper on fire without anyone coming in."

"Won't it cause a fire?" Laney is starting to sound anxious now. I'm a little bit too.

"That's why I'm using the sink," I say. "I'll do the spell,

then turn the water on immediately." I purse my lips. "That won't negate the spell, right?"

"How should I know?" Laney asks. "Ooh! But I know someone who will have matches. I'll meet you at the bathroom in five."

"I'll get paper and a pen." I pick up a napkin with the Headless Horseman on it. "This should work." *I hope.* "See you in a few!"

I look over at Hunter again and see him and his friends whispering and laughing about something as they look at the dance floor. I feel a pang of doubt, but a wave of determination sweeps through me. This is the intention my aunts are always talking about. If there was ever a time to do a spell, it's now. I head to the gym doors and Harry appears, blocking my path.

"Where are you going?" she asks casually. She blows a bright orange bubble with her chewing gum; it matches her tulle skirt that she's paired with a black leotard and tights. "I asked Kevin to play this song just for you and it's almost over." She points at the far corner of the gym. "Hunter's over there."

I knock her hand down. "Shh!" Embarrassment rushes through me, a hot wave. "I can't just *ask* him."

"Why not?"

"Because—" Because what if he says no? What if he laughs at me? What if he leaves me standing there, all night, and I spend another Halloween alone?

"I know it's scary, but trust me, you can't say the wrong thing to the right person. If he's a decent guy, he'll be thrilled if you ask him. And if he's not? Screw him."

I flush. "No, Harry, it has to be perfect. I have a plan."

"A plan?" Harry flashes her green eyes at me under her thick lashes. I decide to be honest. I stand up as tall as I can, only two inches shorter than my sister. "I'm going to cast a small spell. To get *the woodsman* to notice me so I can ask him to dance."

Harry's eyes flicker and I wonder what she's thinking. "Tonight? In front of all these people? Have you even cast a spell before?"

"There's a first time for everything," I say stubbornly, waving the Headless Horseman napkin, which only confuses Harry more.

"Why do you need magic? You're enough, Kat. You don't need magic to get some guy to notice you."

"Yes, I do," I say stubbornly, crossing my arms, which feel cold and prickle with goose bumps—which is odd when the gym is so warm. I can feel my emotions getting the best of me. "I'm not you, Harry."

"What does that mean?" Harry snaps, all knowing and acting wise when she's only eighteen months older.

"He hasn't noticed me yet. But tonight I'll change that," I insist. I look over at the bleachers and realize he's gone. Where did he go? I have to act fast. "I need to go do this. I'll talk to you after, or you'll see us together on the dance floor."

Her mouth twitches. "O-kay." She sounds doubtful and I feel a flash of anger.

"Just go dance with Kevin the Great. I've got this." I spin away from my sister and race for the gym doors. Along the skeleton display framing the entryway, I feel my skirt give a tug. It's caught on something, but I can't see what it is. I fumble to pull my skirt away from the skeletons and shove the doors to get away. That's when I hear the sound of fabric tearing.

I give a small gasp. My skirt has a huge gash from the waist to the mid-thigh on my right side, giving the rest of the world a view of my Supergirl underwear briefs. I quickly clutch both halves of the skirt and pull them together. My eyes meet Harry's. *Help*, I silently say, our disagreement completely forgotten.

She's by my side in less than a breath.

"You can fix this, right? I have to do this spell fast," I beg.

"Yes, yes, yes." Harry pulls me into a darkened classroom. "Let me just think of the spell. Ummmm . . ."

"Don't you know one?"

"I don't know every spell, Kat. I've never ripped my pants before."

"You should by now!"

"I mean, it would help if I had some actual needle and thread that I could infuse with my magic, but . . . let me try this." Harry rips a strip of tulle from her skirt, whispers some words, and crushes it in her palm.

Nothing happens. "It's not working!" I wail.

"Hang on! Give me a second." Harry tries another strip, bigger this time. And then again. By the sixth spell, I've given up all hope, and her skirt has gone from maxi to mini. "This isn't working."

"Then focus!"

"I'm trying, Kat! I'm not perfect. Let's just fix it normally. We'll make it a fashion statement?"

I'm suddenly suspicious. "Why isn't this working? I once saw you mend a hole in your sweater sleeve with *your eyes*."

"I can't do that."

But I know what's going wrong. My sister doesn't *want* to fix my skirt. She has the sacrifice, but not the intention. She'd rather I sit here with my entire butt hanging out than dance with the boy I'm in love with.

My stomach churns as I hear her working below me, somehow having a mountain of safety pins at her disposal that she quickly uses to close the hole. By the time she's done, I have to admit that she's worked it out so well, it looks like a seam in the skirt, and no one will even notice it.

"Come on! Let's get you back out there," Harry says encouragingly. "You don't need some spell to get his attention."

I almost believe her. Besides which, we've been gone too long anyway. Laney is probably looking for me too.

But by the time we rush back into the gym, the dance floor has been taken over by a large group who is doing

"Thriller" in unison, shimmying across the dance floor. I grip Harry's arm in horror when I see who is smack-dab in the middle of the group, staring at each other as if they each hang the moon: Hunter and Zara Patel, dancing together. As I stare, he reaches for her waist and pulls her in to sway as if it's a slow song, even though it totally isn't. She rests her face in his shoulder, as the music transitions to another romantic song.

I gape at them.

"He wasn't worth it, Kat. Trust me," Harry says quietly.

I don't believe her, but I try to stay positive. "It's just one dance."

But it isn't. Hunter and Zara start dating at the dance and are together till the spring, when the whole school learns Hunter is actually dating three girls at the same time. Zara is one of them, and when she finds out, she dumps her protein shake on him in the lunchroom.

I know it's silly, but somehow that hurts more. He had three girlfriends, and that feels like three chances, and he still didn't even look at me.

9

Mystic Hollow Community Page

NEW POST FROM THE DANCE PLACE: If anyone would like to join us to perform at the Halloween carnival, please call the Dance Place. We'll be having practices every day this week and we'd love some newcomers to join us. All ages welcome! No sign-up required.

I stare at my sister as she drags a roller bag and duffel through the hall, marching past me into the kitchen. I haven't seen her since she left for school in August, but she looks good, like always. Her long, blond hair practically shimmers as it moves, like she's in a commercial.

"What are you doing here? You're supposed to be in Boston." I panic, clutching the crystal around my neck out of habit. Despite the growing distance between Harry and me, I see she's still wearing hers too. "Is this about your AirPods charger? Because I swear I didn't take it, and we looked everywhere for it."

"Alexa!" Harry yells, still not talking to me. "Stop!"

The Halloween playlist cuts out, and the house is silent except for its normal creaking as the heat kicks on in protest of this sudden invasion.

"Why am I here?" Harry asks herself and stares at me. "Take a wild guess, Kat." My name sounds bitter on her tongue. "To fix things for you. Again."

I can feel my pulse starting to race, my fingers tingling. Did Mom trick me? "Mom, Dad, and the aunts left me in charge of Samhain. They know I've got the spells covered."

Harry raises her right eyebrow and smiles smugly. "Really?"

I'm so angry, I don't know who to be mad at first: Mom for claiming she trusted me to do the rituals when she didn't, or for my entire family for asking Harry to be my babysitter. Her being here is going to ruin everything I have planned. "You're lying! I'm calling Mom." I rush out of the room to grab my phone from the living room. But the second I spot it on the coffee table, it disappears. I spin around and see Harry has it in her hand. Show-off.

"Do not call Mom." Her voice is eerily calm.

"Give me my phone." I lunge at her as Great-Aunt Aida's portrait glares at us both. Harry smells like cardamom, and her summer tan seems to have faded to a warm glow. This close, I can see a freckle above the right side of her lip, in the same spot I have one. Harry holds the phone out of reach, and a strange feeling comes over me. *She's hiding something.*

"Why are you really here, Harry?" I try to match her calm tone.

Harry hesitates for a second, then drops my phone into my outstretched hand. I hear it rumble with new texts. "Fine. Mom and Dad didn't tell me to come, okay? I did it for the good of Samhain. We both know you can't handle this on your own." She stands there for a minute, then her eyes narrow. "You're having a Halloween party, aren't you?"

Grrrr . . . Harry and her witchy ESP. My heart bangs in my chest, and I try not to give myself away. "No."

"You are!" Harry sounds triumphant. "And it's here on Halloween night when you're supposed to be focusing on the protection spells!"

I crack. "Mom and Dad said I could have one. Everyone will be gone before I cast the spells. I've got it all under control."

"HA!" Harry says, slapping the island counter and sending wooden spoons rolling. "You never have it under control! And then what happens? I have to clean up your mess!"

"You're not my mother, Harry!" I'm shouting now.

"Then stop making me act like one, *Kat*." Her voice is deadly quiet, but I can sense what she's going to do before she does it.

"Don't!" I yell as she grabs a piece of mail on the counter, then rushes to the stove and flips on a burner. The scrap of paper goes up in flames before I can even reach her.

"What did you just burn?" I ask through gritted teeth.

But I have a feeling I know. The invitation that the aunts got to a new show opening. It doesn't matter what it's for—it matters what it was. *An invitation.*

I whip out my phone and scroll through the messages. The evite. The party texts. They're all gone. Harry canceled my party!

"You've ruined everything," I say.

"That was your plan, wasn't it?" Harry asks, guessing perfectly as her nose twitches. "To get a boyfriend. Because I know you don't already have one."

Because who could like Kat Hadley? She doesn't need to say it, but I can all but hear the unspoken words in my head as she smirks at me. She is so smug. I want to knock that stupid smile off her face. My fingernails bite into the palm of my hand with a sharp flicker of pain, and when I draw them back, I can see I punctured the skin in one spot and a tiny needle point of blood rushes up, then drops to the wood floor.

A crash startles us as the knives all leap from their block. Wow, that was . . . sort of something. Not quite what I meant, but the intention was there.

Harry looks at me in surprise. "This is not a game. You know the spells have to be done by two connected souls! You can't do them on your own! What are you trying to do? Break the town's magic?"

How dare she? "This is so typical. The perfect Harriet Hadley trying to swoop in and do everything better than me. Guess what? I don't need you here. I am not trying to break magic! I *know* the protection spells need to be done by two people and they will be! I am doing the rituals with . . . Peter!" Shoot. I almost forgot my fake boyfriend's name. "Who is my boyfriend!"

Harry catches my mistake and her eyes flash. "Your boyfriend, huh?" Harry sneezes, the sound as loud as a gunshot. "Then why has no one met him?"

"The aunts met him yesterday."

Harry's nose wrinkles, like she's about to sneeze again. "Kat, stop lying to me. I know you don't have a boyfriend. You can't!"

I hold my crystal tight, feeling my fingers warm. "Why not! Is it so hard to believe that I found someone who likes me?" I say, and Harry falters.

"I didn't say that," she says hoarsely. "But the boys every Halloween . . . you've always fallen head over heels for a stranger. Someone you don't know, who doesn't know *you.* I just want to protect you."

"Because if someone knew me, they couldn't possibly like me?" I yell back. If she's gunning for a fight, she's going to get one. For the first time in forever, it's just the two of us in this house, and I won't hold back any longer. "And news flash, Harry. I know you feel like I'm your responsibility as your nothing little sister, but you've been gone. You haven't been 'protecting me.' You haven't even been talking to me. I might be invisible at school, but you've made yourself invisible to me."

"That's not true," Harry says, but her voice betrays her. We both know I'm right.

"Just go back to Boston, okay?" I say. "You don't even live here. This isn't your house. Go back to being the perfect daughter with the perfect grades and the perfect hair and the perfect boyfriends. You don't want anything to do with me? Fine. Then don't have anything to do with me. I'm going to get a boyfriend this Halloween. And you can't stop me."

"I already did!" Harry cries.

The phrase seems to hang in the air.

"What?" I ask, my voice low.

"Okay, don't be mad—"

"Harriet Hadley, what did you do?"

"I just wanted to protect you," she says, her voice small, and my larger-than-life sister seems to shrink before my eyes. "You kept picking these . . . losers. Guys who didn't love you, could never love you. And every Halloween I was picking up the pieces of your broken heart. So I cast a spell."

"What did you do," I repeat, my voice low and deadly.

"A spell. To keep you *safe*. So that until you meet the right one, your heart will be protected." Harry swallows thickly. "You can't have a boyfriend, Kat. My spell makes sure of that. Until you meet your soulmate."

"You cast a spell to drive boys away from me?" I screech.

"Not away!" Harry says. "They just . . . won't notice you. It'll keep you safe. I was trying to *protect* you. I'm your older sister."

All my awful Halloweens flash in my mind's eye. All the times I got my heart broken, when my crush ignored me or chose someone else or disappeared without a trace.

"You're not," I whisper.

"Not what?" Harry asks, her eyes going wide.

"My older sister. Because I don't have a sister."

"I was trying to help you! You have no idea what I sacrificed—"

"What *you* sacrificed?" I screech. "You're no one to me, Harry."

"Fine!" she yells, and before I realize it, we're both reaching for the crystals around our necks. The last thing to keep us bonded. "I guess I don't have a sister anymore either!"

Harry and I have always said the same thing at the same time, moved as one, with me just a second behind her. I was always her shadow. But this time, I'm first to rip the crystal from my throat. She mirrors me, and we both throw them down to the flagstones.

They shatter, crystal fracturing into dust. A sudden wind whips through the kitchen, whisking the fragments away.

The air crackles with energy. And that's when I hear an earsplitting sound and look up. A crack snakes across the ceiling above us. It moves fast, plaster falling; Harry and I jump out of the way as the fissure spreads, cutting through a kitchen wall and reaching the floor. I can feel the ground rumbling beneath my feet. The glasses in the cabinet clatter and ring out. Phoebe rushes through the room and stands in front of me now, howling. She never does that.

The whole house is shaking now, and I wonder if we're having an earthquake. But neither Harry nor I move, glaring at each other. Our chests rise and fall, but Harry is the first to crack.

"Look what you did!" she yells. "Mom and Dad are going to kill you!"

"What I did? What you did!" I argue. How am I going to explain this? Sure, my magic has accidentally destroyed some things lately. But the entire house?

Phoebe streaks across the kitchen floor and tries to wedge herself underneath one of the kitchen island stools as the house continues to shake. But at the moment, neither Harry nor I care about the damage. We just glare at each other, then turn in opposite directions to leave the kitchen, each slamming a door behind us.

10

Mystic Hollow Community Page

NEW POST FROM MAYOR CROFT: Mayoral mansion open house Wednesday from 5–7 p.m. to discuss how each of us can do our part to make the town come alive for tourists. I'd like all our fair citizens in attendance. Let's show New England that Mystic Hollow is the destination for Halloween!

You can't have a boyfriend, Kat. I cast a spell.

It's all her fault. Everything.

Harry and I retreat to our rooms across the hall from one another upstairs and both have the same plan: We video chat with Mom and Dad at the airport, where they are waiting for their flight to Florida. Mom picks up my call while Dad clearly picks up Harry's because I can hear both conversations.

"For the last time, I did not tell Harry you needed help with Samhain," Mom says, rubbing her temples. I think our fight is giving her a magic migraine. "But isn't it nice your sister came home to help anyway?"

"I don't need her," I say at the same time Harry says, "I'm not helping her," from her own room across the hall from mine.

"Girls, I hate seeing you two like this," Dad says, and normally it would pull at my heartstrings, but I know what Harry did. Not that I can tell either of my parents. They'll rush home because it means that "Peter" isn't real.

Unless Colton is my soulmate. Which he has to be. I'm sure of it.

My dad is still tripping down memory lane. "It used to be there wasn't a Samhain you two didn't spend together. You had sleepovers all week leading up to the holiday, you were so excited."

"That was a long time ago," I bite out.

"Maybe it's time to re-create the memory," Dad suggests. "You two have the whole house to yourself for Samhain weekend. Why not use it to make some new memories together?"

Harry and I both sigh so loudly from our opposite rooms, I can hear her through the walls and the FaceTime screen. The house creaks loudly as if echoing Dad's sentiment. Downstairs, there's a crash. It seems the magical schism we created in the house is still settling.

"She doesn't need my help, Dad," Harry says. "She made that clear."

"Very clear!" I repeat. "I'm doing the protection spells Saturday with Peter." Who is really Colton. Who now has no clue I was even having a party, thanks to Harry. How am I going to fix all this in time?

Phoebe appears at the edge of my bed and meows mournfully at me, pawing at the wall. Her nails scratch, and I almost swear aloud. The crack running from her nails traces all the way up to my ceiling, and it wasn't caused by a cat. Crap. I knew we had a fissure in the kitchen and the ceiling, but I didn't realize the split ran all the way upstairs. Is it in Harry's room too? What is going on with this house? I need to check the spell book to figure out how to mend the walls.

"Girls!" Mom commands our attention. "I don't know what happened this morning in the hour since your father and I left the house, but I don't care. You two are big girls." Mom's eyes seem to swirl with a rainbow of colors. "You're sisters. Figure this out together!" And then the video cuts out.

Thank goodness. I'm wasting time talking to them, to be honest. As long as Harry leaves me alone, I might be able to salvage this Samhain.

The first step is figuring out how to invite everyone over to my house for a party in . . . three days. On the biggest holiday in Mystic Hollow. I get ready fast and head downstairs, where the back of my neck prickles with the feeling of being watched. I look over at Great-Aunt Aida's portrait.

Is it me or does she look particularly peeved? I pull my coat tightly around me and look at my cat, who has followed me downstairs. "Be good, Phoebs," I whisper, and shut the door behind me.

Walking to school, I pull out my phone. There is a text from the aunts with a picture of Aunt Viv's left arm and Aunt Diane's right ear; a tiny gold broomstick hanging from her lobe. "LOve Theeee Bt!$" says the text, which I take to mean "love the boat." Which is great. This is what I wanted: For my aunts to go away on a six-month cruise so I can have a Halloween party without their meddling. But now? After this fight with Harry and Mom cutting us off, I feel alone. I can't even complain to anyone really about Harry's spell without ruining my plan.

I've been cursed. By my own sister. The idea is so ridiculous and awful I'm not sure if I should laugh or cry.

The wind rustles through the trees, and in the distance, I hear a wolf howl. At least I think it's a wolf. I've never heard one in Mystic Hollow before. In the distance, there are sirens, and then I see a police car rush down the street. Another unfamiliar sight in a town where the only crime is toilet-papering people's homes during sports initiations and Halloween.

Up ahead, I see Laney waiting for me at the edge of Mystic Hollow High's fields, and I walk faster. I have *a lot* to tell her. I bet I could scare her out of her chunky black boots in just one sentence. At whatever face I make, she clutches her book bag to her chest and her "In My Book Girl Era" tee from her mom's store and her eyes go wide. But suddenly my anger fades and a nervous energy seems to wallop me in the face as my hands start tingling.

It's happening again. I shake out my hands. Could this be my magic?

"What's wrong?" I ask.

"It's the weirdest thing," she says, pushing red glasses up onto the bridge of her nose. "I was passing the Crofts' house and there were several police cars out front. Mayor Croft was having a meltdown. Something about an intruder standing at the foot of his bed when he woke up."

"A break-in? In Mystic Hollow?" I can't help sounding skeptical, which I know is foolish. I watch crime shows with my dad sometimes. It's not like Mystic Hollow is immune, even though Mom and the aunts claim we're well protected. It hasn't dawned on me till now that maybe that protection has to do with our Hadley spells.

But it's not Halloween yet. They can't be failing—can they?

"I know! That's what I thought. One of the cops was saying he searched the property and found no one and nothing was taken. I basically hid out behind a scarecrow on the street to listen to the whole conversation. I knew you'd want details."

She's such a good friend. "Did you see Colton?"

Her face falls. "Yes. He's fine. Are you still planning on going to his Halloween party?"

"What?" I rack my brain. There's no way I missed an invitation to a Colton Croft party. "He isn't throwing a party. When is he throwing a party?"

"Halloween," Laney repeats, like I've sprouted two extra heads. "You know, when Halloween parties are. You've been talking about it for weeks. The evite went out back in September." I check my email and see an email from Colton with the subject line: *Killer Halloween Party! (No one will die!)* I click on it and read the details. It's my evite exactly. Down to the time, the food, and the details about the party being outside. It's as if Harry took my whole party and just transferred it over to Colton. Some witch I am. This was one scenario I didn't anticipate. "I can't believe this," I grumble, getting mad at Harry all over again. "That's when my party was supposed to be!"

"Your party? Your parents don't let you throw Halloween parties."

I groan. "Laney, I literally don't have the energy for this."

Laney fidgets, adjusting her jacket with the wind. "Okay . . ."

"I'm serious!" I sigh. Laney is my closest friend. If I can't talk to her, I'm truly alone. "I know you don't remember, but that's because of magic. Harry found out about the party and did a spell to cancel it and make everyone forget."

Laney pulls at a strand of her own dark hair. "Are you saying Harry cast a spell on me?" I nod. "I can't believe her!" she says, sounding outraged on my behalf, for which I'm glad. She frowns.

"What?"

"So what are you going to do about the rituals? I know you need your one true love. If you can't get Colton to your house for Halloween—"

"I'll get him there," I say.

"I think you should call Harry. Have her call her boyfriend. The one she dumped right after Halloween her senior year. What was his name? Jack?"

I pull at a loose thread on my quilted coat and watch the stitching unravel. "I don't need perfect Harry to cast her perfect spell with her perfect boyfriend. I'm going to do it. With Peter."

"Who's Peter? Seriously, Kat, you are not making sense."

"I mean Colton!" I cry. I stomp away and then wait for Laney to catch up. We're going to be late for school at this rate.

Laney thinks for a moment. "If it makes you feel any better, Mayor Croft seemed really upset about the intruder. Maybe Colton will cancel his party—"

I brighten. "Yes! I mean, I'm not thrilled about the break-in, but maybe you're right. Then I can offer to have the party at my house where there are no chaperones, and Colton will think I've saved Halloween." I warm at the thought of Colton and me greeting people at my front door. Now all I have to do is get rid of Harry.

We've reached the school parking lot. Kids are pouring into school, walking or getting off buses. I see Colton and two friends getting out of a car together. "I just need to find a way to get him alone, but we don't have the same lunch period and the only class we have together is chemistry. I'm not doing it there."

"Definitely not." Laney purses her lips. "What about stopping by his house? We can do some investigating and maybe float the idea of you hosting."

"Laney, you are brilliant!" Maybe I don't have my sister in my life, but I do have the next closest thing to it. I reach up to touch my crystal out of habit and remember. It's shattered in a million pieces in the kitchen. My hands tingle in response to the thought. I try to push my sadness away. I don't need Harry or the crystal. I can do this on my own.

11

Mystic Hollow Community Page

NEW POST FROM MAYOR CROFT'S OFFICE: Due to an unforeseen issue at the mansion, tonight's meeting is canceled.

COMMENT FROM SOCCER DAD12: Saw the mayor run screaming from his mansion this a.m. What's going on?

COMMENT FROM GIVEBROOKIEACOOKIE: I heard the sheriff was called in about a ghost sighting.

COMMENT FROM SOCCERDAD12: What? LOL! Can't wait to see whatever video he's working on!

After school, I follow Colton to the town green, but instead of going home, he heads to Witches Brew. I guess he's enjoying football practice being canceled for Hallo-week. Unfortunately, everyone else is also at Witches Brew.

"You okay there, Hadley?" Zach asks, stopping by my

table and looking down at my notebook. He's wearing a navy-blue Henley today and green cords like he's auditioning to be in a fall advertisement for Mystic Hollow. "It's not like you to do your homework here where I can see your answers."

I take a sip from my frosted mug, enjoying the bite of the sugar rim. Today Zach handed me an apple cider before I even asked. It's exactly what I needed. "How do you know I'm not writing down the wrong answers so you'll copy them and fail?"

Zach's lips tug up slightly on one side. "Like you'd ever write down the wrong answers."

"True," I admit, sip the last of my cider, and wave my glass at him. "Does this come with free refills?"

He rolls his eyes. "You didn't pay for the first fill."

"Please?" I ask sweetly. He sighs heavily and takes the cup. I call after him. "Don't forget to refresh the sugar rim!"

Zach takes the empty mug back to the window where his brother Landon is working. I see Landon say something I can't hear. "Shut it," Zach says as he returns with my drink.

I accept it with a grin. "No whipped cream?" I tease.

"Don't push it, Hadley." But for some reason, he's smiling too. He pulls a rag out of his pocket and cleans off the table for me, which has sugar crystals on it from my previous drink. "So what really brings you in today? Hoping to talk to someone special?"

"Actually, I am," I say, glancing over at Colton.

Zach squeezes his eyes shut for a moment. "Don't tell me you're going to his party too. I thought you were going to have one."

I sit up straight. "You remember me wanting to throw a Halloween party?"

He gives me a look. "Uh, yeah? You only mentioned it a thousand times in chem class. What happened?"

Over in the corner, Colton is completing his goodbye rituals with his teammates, which involves a lot of hand clasping and slapping. "I am still going to have a party. I just need to talk to Colton first." I gulp down my second cider. "Thanks for the refill," I say, standing up fast and tripping over my chair.

Zach grabs my arm to steady me. He's standing so close, I can smell the Altoid on his breath. "Thanks," I say, even though I can feel my stomach doing backward flips. How have I never noticed his lashes were so long?

"Excuse me," says someone with a wisp of a voice. Zach and I are still standing close as we look over at a trio of women with long, dark hair that trails all the way down their long, black dresses. They could be in a black-and-white filter, except for their bloodred lips. "Is it true these are the very grounds the Headless Horseman is buried on?"

"That's the rumor," Zach says, adopting a pleasant customer service tone to his voice as he lets go of my arm. "But no one knows for sure."

The women continue staring at us, and I feel my hands tingling. My *magic*. There's something odd about this trio. "You might want to try Spirited Books," I suggest. "They have books on the town history and the Headless Horseman."

"Thank you," the one in the middle says as the other two women stare at the people in line. Then they turn as one and seemingly glide away.

We both look at each other. "Tourists," we say at the same time.

"That was weird," Zach says, thinking what I'm feeling. "Speaking of odd, have you seen Ronald today?"

"Ronald? You mean Fred?"

"It's Ronald. And yes. Normally he comes by at least once, but he hasn't touched the food I left out for him. I hope he's okay." Zach looks out across the green, which is filling with booths for the Halloween carnival. "It's supposed to rain tonight."

It's sweet how much Zach cares about this dog. I find myself smiling again but quickly hide it before he can see. "I'm sure he's fine. If I see him on my way over to Colton's, I'll let you know—aaah!" I scream as a boy around our age pops up in front of us. His face is muddy and he's got leaves in his brown hair, which is sticking up like his eyebrows. His eyes are wild as he smiles excitedly.

"HEY! HI THERE! HI! HELLO!"

Zach instinctively steps in front of me. "Hey. Can I help you?"

The guy looks back and forth, panting. "Are you going on a walk? Can I come? Can I? CAN I? I need to run! Run!" He's bouncing around now.

"Um, go for it," Zach says, gesturing out the door at the beautiful fall day. The sun shines. Leaves tumble. A squirrel goes bounding past.

"OH BOY!" the boy screams, and he takes off out the door.

"Thanks for the apple cider," I say, backing away from a very confused-looking Zach. "I owe you one."

"You owe me many!" Zach yells as I cross the green, headed for Spirited Books. Laney is waiting outside the store when I arrive.

"You just missed the weirdest tourists," she says. "They just stood in the doorway and kept asking if they could come inside." She fidgets with the beads on her wrist. "And one of them kept looking at me and licking her lips."

"I think Mayor Croft might be appealing to some very strange people. There was this hairy, dirty boy—"

"Are vampires real?" Laney asks abruptly.

Yes, I almost say. But it doesn't matter that vampires exist *somewhere*. There are no vampires in Mystic Hollow. The Hadley protection spells prevent that. Plus, the rest of the world doesn't know they're real and I'd like to keep it that way. "You read too many horror novels," I say, even though I can't hide my shiver.

"You're probably right. Their skin was just so pale, and

their lips were so red," she says as we walk.

We only make it two houses before we hear shouting. When we look over at the town green, the strange boy who approached me and Zach is racing across the green with someone's football—which would be normal, only he has it gripped in his teeth. A group of boys is trying to catch him to no avail. "It's almost Halloween, I guess?" Laney offers.

"Right," I say as we reach the Croft mansion. My aunts always turn their nose up at the style of the Croft home, but I like their Victorian. It's painted white and teal, with a low picket fence lined with yellow and orange mums, and there are always candles burning in the windows. Except today.

"Are you sure they're home?" Laney asks. "It looks dark inside."

"I just saw Colton leave Witches Brew," I say as I step up to the door and use the brass knocker.

The door opens so fast, the wreath flies off the door. An older woman with salt-and-pepper hair rushes past us, muttering to herself. From the open door comes a rush of cold air. Laney and I both rub our arms to keep warm.

And then the woman rushes to her van out front. It's bright purple, and the sunlight glints off the cheerful letters that read: *Spirit Sweepers.*

"Kat," Laney whispers, pointing at the back as it races off down the quiet street, nearly hitting a pumpkin display on the corner.

Sleep tight. We fight all sprites.

"Is that an *exorcist*?" Laney whispers.

I step into the subzero house. It feels like walking into a freezer. "Nonsense. Probably just a ghost hunter."

Laney's eyes are as big as dinner plates. "Is that better? Do you think Mayor Croft saw a ghost?"

No, I don't. Only witches can see ghosts, and the wards make sure that ghosts can't even fully manifest.

"Oh, that must be Colton's dad. I'm sure he'll set us straight," I say, pointing to the figure by the window. His shoulders are broad, his hair salt-and-pepper. "Excuse me, Mr. Mayor?"

The figure turns. His face is gnarled and grizzled, but it's not the face that bothers me. It's the fact that I can see the curtains straight *through* it.

"Kat," Laney whispers again.

"Sorry, I guess no one's home," I say, gently backing up.

Laney hits my arm. "Kat, is that . . . is that . . . *a ghost*?"

12

Mystic Hollow Community Page

NEW POST FROM CRESSIDA MONROE: Warning! Keep your pets inside! I've been hearing wolves howling all afternoon.

NEW COMMENT FROM ANONYMOUS: There are no wolves in Connecticut! You must be hearing coyotes. Is it a full moon or something?

"You can see him too?" I ask Laney. If Laney is seeing them too, something is wrong.

"Yeah," she says, sounding nervous and excited at the same time. "Hello."

But she isn't looking at the older man by the window. There's another ghost coming down the stairs.

"Greetings," says the young man as he glides down to us. He can't be more than twenty. I try to place his time period, but it's hard when he's wearing a white shirt and pants with dress shoes—1800s, maybe? "It's good to make your acquaintance, Miss . . . ?"

"Laney," I say since Laney's jaw is wide open. "I'm Katherine. We were just . . . leaving." This is bad. This is really bad. I need to call—

I can't tell my aunts. I can't tell my parents. And I definitely can't tell Harry. I have to handle this by myself.

My mom's spell book should have the answers. I need to get home.

"She's looking for Colton," Laney volunteers.

"Colton?" comes another voice. Two ghosts pop out of the wall and float toward us. One is older, a woman, and one is a boy. They're dressed almost identically. That's when it dawns on me. The mayor didn't see an intruder this morning—he saw ghosts!

"You can do much better than Colton, dear," says the motherly-looking ghost. "Frankly an embarrassment to the Croft name. Our descendant, singing in the rain room as he cleans his behind."

I did not need to know that. I feel myself blush.

The young ghost nods. "But I must say, that Taylor Shift is catchy."

"Swift," Laney and I correct him.

"A pity he didn't get the height from my side of the family," the stately-looking ghost by the window says in a deep voice. "Always adding that padding into his shoes to appear taller. Disgraceful."

Colton wears lifts?

"Well, thank you for all this. We should really be going."

I grab Laney's arm and head toward the door. I need to get home and get rid of these ghosts before Colton and his dad decide to get out of town to somewhere much less haunted.

The younger ghost waves. "You're welcome to return later. We have many more embarrassing stories about our heir. Why, the other morning, he spent nearly an hour crafting his hair—"

I pull the door closed behind us. On the street, I see the strange pale women from earlier. They huddle close together and are whispering. Something is definitely going on.

"Now what?" Laney asks. "You've got to find Colton and talk to him about the party before it's too late. We definitely need that ritual done, like, yesterday."

"I know." I pull a small slip of paper out of my pocket and the matches I took this morning from the house. I look at the words I've written as an intention. *Let me host Colton's party*. I light the match and let the words burn.

The wind whistles through the trees and I look around, hoping to see some sign the spell worked. Like Colton appearing, but there's nothing. I sigh.

Then my phone begins to buzz. It's not Colton. "It's my aunts." I feel slightly ill. If they're calling from the ship, this is bad. *They know I used magic. They know about the ghosts. And possible vampires*. I let it ring. Seconds later, a voicemail appears on my phone. I press Play.

"Kat, is something going on that we should know about?" Aunt Viv's voice is clear.

"Tell her we know!" Aunt Diane whispers.

Aunt Viv shushes her. "Did you use magic to get us these tickets? Because this boat isn't going to the Bahamas. It's headed to Bermuda. We know something is wrong. And they say we have phone service now, but once we reach the triangle, they expect—" *Click*.

I need to get the family spell book and fix this.

13

Mystic Hollow Community Page

NEW POST FROM ANONYMOUS: Is it me or are the tourists getting weirder? What's with the three women wandering around town asking about the grave site of the Headless Horseman?

When I get home, I hear Harry screaming.

As mad as I am at her, my sisterly reflex kicks in. "Harry!" I run toward the sound of her voice and find her in the dining room standing in front of a wall with a huge fissure. Harry's got a broken bottle of glue in her hand and is watching wallpaper all around the room peel off the walls.

"What did you do?" I cry, rushing over to a wall and trying to stop the damage. My mom loves this wallpaper. The burgundy floral design is over a hundred years old, and now it's disintegrating in front of our eyes, peeling like an apple.

"I did a mending spell," Harry says, dropping to the floor to try to gather all the wallpaper slivers. "I do them all the time! It's what I use on my hair, but something is wrong. Instead of fixing the walls, it's destroying them even more. What are we going to do? This spell always works!" She sounds really upset, and I'm about to make her more so.

"You use it on your hair, and it *always works*?" I ask, biting back a laugh. Her normally sleek hair is a big ball of frizz, the edges fried. She has split ends aplenty.

Harry grabs her head and starts patting it. "What? No! Is it a mess?" She jumps up, dropping the wallpaper pieces and rushing to the dining room mirror. She screams even louder. "What's wrong with my hair?"

"I don't know," I ask, fascinated by this turn of events. The perfect Harriet Hadley has bad hair! My heart practically sings for a moment, and I can hear my father tsking me from hundreds of miles away ("*You're sisters! You should support each other.*") "Did you do a spell?" I ask innocently. Of course she did. She's done spells on her hair for years and never revealed what they were.

Harry ignores me and shrieks again in frustration. "Why is the enchantment failing?"

"Do you want me to try your enchantment to try to fix your hair?" I offer, tucking a strand of my healthy red hair behind my ear.

Harry's head whips around so fast, I think it's spinning. "You can't fix this. You can barely handle your own spells." Her expression falters. "No. Kat. I'm sorry. I didn't mean—"

"Maybe," I cut her off, my anger returning, "you're the one who can't handle your spells. Look what's happened to the dining room!" I say, looking around at the fallen wallpaper. "And the cracks in the walls! You did something to cause this!" The house, if I'm not imagining it, seems to settle with a heavy creak.

"Me?" Her eyes narrow. "How do you know this isn't because you did a spell wrong! Did you try to resend your party evite? Maybe that's what caused the house to go haywire."

She marches out of the dining room into the hall. I follow her. Then I hear a sniff and look up. Great-Aunt Aida's portrait expression has changed again. Now it looks like she's crying.

"Well, thanks to you, Colton is now the one having a party!"

"Good!" Harry yells. "We don't need people coming over here. We've got enough problems right now."

"Problems caused by you," I say.

Harry glares at me under her frizzy, wild hair. "I canceled a party. Why would that break the house?" she asks, but she sounds nervous as she walks into the kitchen.

"The nexus," comes a voice, and we both jump.

There's a girl in a bonnet and floral dress our own age sitting at the kitchen island. Her skin is translucent, and I can see through her chest to the stove clock, which is flashing 12:00. Funny because my alarm clock was flashing that this morning too. Did the power go out?

"Kat, go get the family spell book," Harry whispers. "Because I'm seeing a ghost in our kitchen."

"Psshh," I reply, unfazed. "This is like the sixth ghost I've seen today."

Harry looks at me incredulously.

"What are you going to do, exorcise her?"

"Maybe," Harry snaps.

"Excuse me," the girl says. "Please don't exorcise me. This is my house too."

Harry pinches her nose, holding back a sneeze. "You're a Hadley."

She nods. "Eleanor Hadley. Pleased to make your acquaintance."

"I think I'm named after you," I say excitedly. "My name is Katherine Eleanor Hadley."

"To be remembered in such a fashion is a compliment," Eleanor says, then looks up at the ceiling with a frown. "I died in this house the first winter it was built. It was a bad winter. Although it seems you're in for a worse one."

"Sorry to hear that," Harry says.

"I've made my peace with my passing," Eleanor says matter-of-factly. "Though I do like returning at Samhain to watch Hadley magic at its finest. People believe Harold Croft is the founder of Mystic Hollow, but it's my grandmother, Beatrice Shannon Hadley." She smiled wickedly. "That's why we placed Beatrice's spell book and some of her crystals inside the base of the monument after her passing. That monument belongs as much to the Hadleys as it does the Crofts," she insists, and points a finger at me. "Please tell me you two are not this year's casters." She frowns.

"You think the house falling apart is our fault?" Harry says, taking it personally.

Eleanor's smile is thin. "The location of this house is no accident. Our foremothers built it atop the nexus of magic in Mystic Hollow. If the house is falling apart, magic itself could be failing."

"We didn't break the house," Harry says stiffly, crossing her arms.

"We sort of did," I mutter under my breath.

Harry gives us a look. "I know what my intention was. And it wasn't to do anything to the house."

Okay, so that's the Harry Hadley glare.

"A house is not just four walls and a roof," Eleanor says carefully.

"She doesn't even live here," I say, but my hands tingle with my magic, like it knows better.

Harry won't look at me. "Kat's right. This isn't my home. Because she's *not* my family."

The floor starts to shake again and the next thing I know, a crack has split the kitchen island in half. A whoosh of cold air and snow rises from inside the fissure. Harry and I look at each other and bolt from the room.

"What just happened?" I cry. "Did you do magic?"

"No, did you?" Harry argues. I shake my head.

And then both of our phones start to ring.

"It's Aunt Diane," I whisper, my heart pounding.

Harry looks at her phone too. "It's Aunt Viv trying to FaceTime."

Neither of us are brave enough to pick up. We let the calls go to voicemail.

"A crack in the foundation can send every wall tumbling down," Eleanor says wisely, drifting through the wall.

Harry and I look at one another, and then she snatches up the family spell book, darting down into the basement. I reach up for my crystal and remember it's destroyed and rush upstairs just to be away from her, leaving Eleanor alone to haunt the foyer.

Boys of Halloween Past

CRUSH #3: JUSTIN TREMBLE
THE YEAR: NINTH GRADE

"Kat, some kid just knocked over an entire tray of drinks. Can you help with cleanup?" asks my Haunted House of Hamburgers' manager, Chris. He's balancing two trays of haunted hamburger sliders. At the Haunted House of Hamburgers, every food is spooky. These hamburgers have skulls burned into the buns.

"Got it!" I jump off the ice machine in the kitchen where I've been taking my break and head for the mop and cleanup rags. I'm going to need a ton.

You'd think a Halloween-themed restaurant would be a seasonal thing, but Mystic Hollow is Halloween-themed year-round. People around here can't get enough of it. There are Halloween animatronics in a pretend playground out front, different scary movies playing on each TV, and old-timey portraits with eyes that follow customers around the room. This year, Chris added a soundtrack of thunder with strobe lights in the ceiling, and the "lightning" flashes always catch me by surprise.

At fifteen, I am too young to waitress, but after my begging, Chris finally broke down and hired me to bus tables this past summer. I've been determined to make enough money to buy the latest MacBook after I heard Zach talking about how it'll make his study guides "next level." When I get it first, it'll supercharge my studying instead, and I'll kick off my high school career by ranking first in the grade. Except lately, I haven't been keeping tabs on my earnings. I've been asking for shifts for a different reason.

Justin Tremble groans when he sees me with the mop. "Oh no, you're the sacrifice for table five?" He's holding his order pad in one hand and a dish of half-eaten tomato caprese bites—made to look like googly eyeballs—in the other. "Let me put in this order, and I'll help you. Don't want you drowning in that spill, seriously."

My heart soars. Justin wants to help me again. He's always offering to help me refill the toilet paper in the bathrooms, bus my tables when the restaurant is so packed I can't keep up, and last week, when a customer started yelling at me that their order was taking too long (something I have nothing to do with), he jumped in and defended me. Plus, he's two years older, and the only high schooler (aside from my sister) who I really know.

So of course I'm in love with him.

I stare after him as he heads to deliver the order. He cuts above the crowd, the sort of broad shoulders that rival our quarterback's. Because it's his job, Justin is extroverted—he lingers at the table, laughing and joking, just enough for me to spot his dimples. When a girl asks him about the buttons on his work apron, he shows the cheesy blinking Halloween buttons off with pride. He's nice, he's gorgeous, and he loves Halloween.

In other words, he's perfect for me.

And since it's the most romantic night of the year for me—us—I'm going to tell him tonight and make this our first of many Halloweens together.

In that moment, Justin looks over at me, and that smile, it isn't about his job. It's just for me.

Goose bumps race down my back as thunder booms through the speakers. *Focus, Kat!* I tell myself, heading to the truly massive spill. Cleaning it up doesn't take long because my mind is elsewhere. I've decided I'm going to write Justin a note about how I feel and ask him out to eat somewhere other than Haunted House of Hamburgers. As I finish with the spill, Chris gestures for me to bus a nearby table. Justin is taking orders at the table next to it, and when he finishes, he stops by, his pen tucked behind his ear. Thankfully, I'm almost done clearing off the table.

"Need me to send out a lifeboat?"

I don't even have to force my laugh. "I made it back to shore." I hold up the bus tub as proof and pray I don't have any ketchup on my apron. My eyes move to the order pad in Justin's apron pocket, and I wonder: Is there a spell I can try to get that pad? There are plenty of ways to sacrifice items in a diner. With no tables to bus for a minute, I make my move. My mom has been sitting me down for weekly witching lessons, and while I still haven't managed to do much of anything, I'm starting to understand that I have to give something to get something. Maybe it has to be something meaningful, not just something that represents the item.

I duck into the bag and pull my friendship diary out of my bag. I pull out a page and write my message, my hands shaking: *I've been wanting to say something to you for a long time: I like you. Any chance you'd want to get dinner sometime. Anywhere but here? —Kat* And then I approach the deep fryer.

"Sorry, Laney," I mutter. Then I hold it tight, thinking as hard as I can: *Make my note appear in his pocket.*

And I let go. The diary hisses when it meets the hot oil. Before my eyes, it begins to disintegrate, flaking into nothingness.

"What are you doing!" comes a voice.

I startle and then groan. Ashton, Chris's super-annoying thirteen-year-old nephew, is standing there, hands on his hips.

"Nothing, Ashton," I say.

"I definitely saw you put your book in the deep fryer," Ashton says, his voice nearing screeching levels that only bats could hear. "I'm going to tell my uncle—"

He steps over, but the book is gone.

I hold my breath. Did the spell work?

"Like I said," I say, trying to hide how breathless I suddenly feel. "Nothing."

And then I wait.

I clean a table where a kid puked after stuffing too many fries in his mouth.

I deal with Tom Callabra's table after they have a ketchup fight.

I pass Justin a thousand times. He says, "Hi," "How's it going?" and "T-minus one hour till shift's over," but nothing about my note. I start to feel sick to my stomach. Even if he doesn't like me, he wouldn't just ignore the note, would he?

As I am bussing my final table, staring out the window and fantasizing about introducing Justin to my parents, I glance out the front window and there he is. My heart drops. His arm is around Emma Lansing, a senior at Mystic Hollow High. When he catches me staring, he raises a hand in a sarcastic salute.

They head to Emma's car and she turns, giving me a dirty look.

I focus on the table, trying to hide how hurt I feel. Would he really read my note and not say anything? I'm not sure what to think. Then I feel a tap on my shoulder. And there's Ashton.

"Don't worry," I say automatically. "I've been waiting the mandatory thirty seconds for the—"

Ashton slides my note across the newly cleaned tabletop.

I glance up in surprise.

"Where did you get that?"

"Found it in my apron pocket," he says with a smile full of metal. When he gives me an exaggerated wink, his bowl cut flutters.

What did my magic do?

Ashton steps closer and raises his eyebrows suggestively. "I'm not usually interested in older women, but for you, I'd be willing to make an exception."

14

Mystic Hollow Community Page

NEW POST FROM MICHELLE JARVUS: Best Halloween gag I've ever seen: A skeleton at Witches Brew drinking a pumpkin spice latte that spills right through him!

COMMENT FROM HEATHER VERR: Wow! And I thought the bat I just saw "transform" into a woman in front of the dance studio was a great trick. Mystic Hollow has definitely upped their Halloween game this year!

Harry and I spend the rest of Wednesday night avoiding each other. Apparently, she thinks Eleanor was being very literal and has been disappearing to the basement and the outside of the house to check the foundation. Meanwhile, I know what Eleanor meant: the wards. I need to make sure we are ready to cast them, and by *we*, I mean me and Colton, who is clearly my true love. I fall asleep with my social studies book on top of me and wake up to daylight. My alarm clock is flashing

12:00 again so I find my phone. It's 8:03 a.m.! I'm late for school!

I jump out of bed and rush into the hall to use the bathroom and crash into Harry coming out of her room at the same time. If possible, her hair has gotten frizzier.

"Sorry," we say at the same time. "My alarm didn't go off," we add in unison.

Jinx! I want to shout like we always did as kids.

Mom said we've always had an uncanny ability to say the exact same thing at the same time, as if we're reading each other's minds. I thought that ability was lost, but now I wonder. I feel a glimmer of hope. Then Harry has to go and ruin it.

"At least I'm not late for school," she says smugly.

I glare at her. "Thanks, Captain Obvious," I say, my bitterness returning. I brush past her. "Get out of my way so I can get ready."

"Well, I need to get in there too. I've got an important meeting soon." Harry tries to squeeze into the bathroom we share, and we both get stuck in the doorjamb.

"What's your meeting?" I ask. When Harry only blushes, I shriek. "Oh, who is it with? Who is it with, Harry?"

"Shut up, Kat," she grumbles. "None of your business."

"Then I get the bathroom first!"

I try to push past her, my elbow poking her rib cage; her right arm coming dangerously close to jabbing me in the throat. Then both our phones start ringing at the same time. The ringtone is the same too. "Witchy Woman" by the Eagles. We look at each other.

"Mom and Dad," we say in unison, and break out of the bathroom, racing for our phones. We've always had the same ringtone for our parents. I had no idea Harry still used it. My call is from Dad. I bring my phone out to the hall; Harry lingers in the threshold to her bedroom, Mom's face splashed across her phone screen.

"It is a witch's job to answer their calling," Eleanor says smugly as she floats up the stairs. I flinch. Okay, so whatever is going on with the wards didn't magically fix itself overnight. "Also, it's rude to ignore one's family."

Without meaning to, I share a glare with Harry: *Can you believe this girl?* We both seem to remember that we're mad at each other at the same time and turn back to our phones. I put Dad on speaker as Harry does the same with Mom. "Hi!" we say in unison in our fakest cheerful voices.

"Why are you both ignoring your aunts?" Mom demands by way of greeting. "Don't you realize how expensive it is to call from the ship?"

"Hi, Mom! Nice to hear from you too," I say pleasantly. "How are Grams and Grampa?"

"Katherine Eleanor Hadley, do not start with me," she says.

Eleanor floats closer. "That's my name!" she says excitedly.

Harry freezes and I hold my breath, wondering if Mom can hear her.

But Mom doesn't say anything about the phantom voice. "I have had a migraine since yesterday afternoon. I know something is going on at the house. I want both of you to tell me what is going on right now."

I can't help but flick my eyes to Harry's, but once again she bites her lip and looks away, as Eleanor watches us both like this is the best entertainment she's had in centuries.

"What your mother means is that as Hadleys, your responsibility isn't just to cast the wards every year," Dad says like he's in lecture, and I feel the beginning of a chill up the back of my neck. "Our family is the conduit for magic. And family isn't just one person."

"For centuries, the Hadley bond is what has made Mystic Hollow so powerful. A powerful force for *good*," Mom interrupts. "And if you're lying to us about—"

"We just want to make sure you two don't have a problem you can't handle on your own," Dad cuts in gently, ever the diplomat. "Remember, Mystic Hollow isn't just our town. It's our home. And we must protect our home."

Harry and I both shift uncomfortably. Neither one of us wants to tell them that the house seems to be splitting in two and Mom's beloved wallpaper looks like it went through a shredder.

"Everything is fine, Mom," Harry says. "I'm performing

the rituals on Samhain. I reached out to Jack to get coffee. We're meeting later this morning."

I bristle. So Harry is taking over? She thinks her ex is more likely to be her true love than Colton is to be mine? "That's too kind of her," I say, as fake as I can. "But the spell requires true love. And thankfully, what Peter and I have . . . is real."

Harry mutters under her breath, "Just about as real as he is."

I whirl to her, ready to snap, when there's a tinkling about. That's our only warning before the hallway chandelier comes crashing down between us. A cloud of dust—and thankfully nothing else—billows out.

We stand there in shock, grateful to be unscathed, until we hear, "What was that!"

"Mom, calm down," Harry says.

"Nothing!" I say quickly.

"You'd tell us if something was going wrong, wouldn't you? Harry?" I can hear the worry in Mom's voice, but it does piss me off that she's relying on my sister and not me.

"We're fine," Harry says, her voice steely.

"Good," Mom allows, and from her tone I can tell she's trying to massage away another headache building in her temples. "Because Grams and I both have the strangest feeling something is happening with the magic in Mystic Hollow."

If what Dad said is right and our house channels all of

the magic, maybe Harry and I didn't just break the house. Maybe we broke the magic itself.

Which can't be the case. That isn't even possible.

Right?

"Everything is fine," Harry says curtly, kicking a bit of the chandelier into my shin. It leaves a long, dusty stripe on my pajama pants and I grit my teeth, holding back a scream. "You just enjoy spending time with Grams and Grampa."

Mom is quiet for a moment. "All right. Just remember: You can lie to me, but your intentions always come through in your magic." I feel a pit in my stomach. "Call if you hear anything odd."

"Will do! Love you!" Harry and I chorus. Then we hang up at the same time.

"Perhaps you shouldn't have ended that call," Eleanor says. "Because there is certainly something 'odd' going on in the kitchen."

Harry and I glower at one another. Her mouth opens, and I can almost hear the sweet, sweet apology, but then I remember that she literally cast a curse on me and is going behind my back to meet with her ex to steal this Halloween from me and Colton. So I shove my way into the bathroom, slamming the door in her face.

I wait for her outrage, but for some reason, I only hear Harry go back into her room. With a triumphant sigh, I reach for my toothbrush, propping my phone up on the sink. That's when I see all the messages:

Chris Haunted Hamburgers:

Can you come in this afternoon? Someone called out. 3:30 to closing?

Laney:

Where are you?

Did you also lose power?

What the heck is going on with the clocks? Did you cast another spell?

Do you think they're gonna cancel school? Almost no one showed up. I bet you're still sleeping.

I wonder if they'll send us home.

Zach:

Hadley, you picked the wrong day to be absent. I heard Mr. Ruth is going to give everyone extra credit just because he doesn't know what to do with us during class.

That means my grade will be higher than yours, if that wasn't clear.

Just as I'm about to send a snarky text to Zach, a new text comes through.

Colton:

Hey you. A little birdy told me you were planning to throw a Halloween party the same night as me. That's totally not cool 😼

Because that would mean you weren't coming to mine.

So I'm moving mine to Friday.

You'd better come 😼

I blink hard. "What in the name of Samhain is going on?" I ask myself, just as the lights in the house flicker and go out.

15

Mystic Hollow Community Page

NEW POST FROM GAIL MATHERS: Was anyone else woken up this morning by screeching? Looked out my window and saw this thing with wings and red eyes swooping over my yard! Between this and the wolf sightings, keep your dogs and cats inside!

NEW COMMENT FROM ERIC SABEL: Sure you didn't dream of Mothman last night?

With school canceled, the house falling apart, and Harry apparently deciding now is the perfect time to go on a date, taking my boss up on his offer for an extra shift doesn't sound like the worst idea. It quickly becomes the best idea when Laney texts me that everyone from school is going to Haunted House of Hamburgers. Including Colton.

And Chris is extra grateful when I show up early, because Haunted House of Hamburgers is packed. The restaurant is one of the few places in town that has power, and everyone seems to be looking for a place to charge their phones and get a hot meal.

"Kat, thank god," Chris says when he sees me. He hands me a wash basin full of dirty dishes. "I think I've run out of hamburgers. Can you believe how many people are here?"

"Happy Halloween, I guess," I say, resting the tub on my hip and looking around. I feel the hair on my neck stand up as if I'm being watched. I try to shake it off, but my hands have started buzzing—does that mean it's something magical? "After I run these to the kitchen, where do you need me?"

"Think you can wait tables instead of bussing?" Chris says hopefully, and thrusts a notepad at me.

I fumble it in shock, trying not to drop the dirty dishes. "Am I even allowed?"

"Kat, I'm gonna be honest," Chris says, sounding manic, as he takes back the bin he just handed me barely a minute ago. "Tucker didn't call out. He walked off. I know Mayor Croft has been trying to get tourists here, but these Halloween enthusiasts are just too much. Some guy in the bathroom is dressed as a winged bat. And that guy at the bar? I know he and his friends are all dressed as skeletons, but I can see his *skull*. His *skull*, Kat. And if that wasn't bad enough, there is a table of women in the back who look like death. They keep asking about the Headless Horseman."

I still. Could it be the women from yesterday? Something doesn't sit right with me about all these visitors. Especially the winged bat. That can't be real, can it? Chris sounds like he's describing Mothman and that's impossible. Mom said Mothman hasn't been seen since the 1960s when a coven in Virginia sent him to the underworld.

I scan the restaurant. Sure, a lot of my classmates are here. Colton, I'm pleased to see, is over in the corner with Tom Callabra and the rest of the jocks. They even brought a football and are tossing it around inside. Normally, that would be enough to earn a speech from Chris, but today he doesn't even seem to have noticed. And I can see why. That's definitely Mothman huddled by the bar, clutching onto one of the pendant lights. Those girls in the darkest corner are probably vampires, considering those red drinks are most likely not the Shrieking Shirley Temples. And yep, those are actual skeletons at the bar. No costume could be that good.

The wards are supposed to keep all these things out. Why does it feel like instead they've all been drawn here? Like Mystic Hollow has become some sort of . . . supernatural magnet?

"Why don't you take five and get some air," I tell Chris. "I'll handle the tables."

"Five. Yes. Thanks. *Skulls*," he mutters to himself as he walks away, bumping into someone hairy, dirty, and familiar. The guy's eyes light up when he sees me.

"Girl! Girl with boy! Do you have any treats? Ronald

Fred wants a treat! Treat! Treat!"

I freeze. "Did you say Ronald *Fred*?"

"Heads!" Tom Callabra yells, and that's my only warning as the football sails over me. I hunch down, trying to protect my face, but the dirty boy is taking off after it, leaping into the air to try to catch it with his *mouth.*

"Hey, it's Kat!" Colton calls, waving at me. I walk over, confused. "Scoot over, guys, make some room for her." When no one moves, he glares, his voice dropping. "I'm serious. Do it."

"Uh," I say, "has anyone taken your order?"

"Are you on the menu?" Colton asks, winking.

I stare open-mouthed.

"Sorry," he says quickly, as his friends guffaw and Tom lets out a low *yooooo.* "I mean, did you see my texts? Are you coming to my party? It was pretty cool of me to move mine, right?"

Did you find his resting place?

The voice speaks directly into my head, like someone jammed a headphone into my skull. I flinch and turn around only to find one of the strange women with long black hair standing far too close. "How did you get across the room that fast?" I whisper.

Did you find the Headless Horseman's resting place? she says in my head again, and jerks her lips up in a robotic smile. Baring her fangs.

Right. They're one hundred percent vampires. Vampires, in Mystic Hollow. Like the wards don't exist. Vampires in the middle of a crowded restaurant. Haunted House of Hamburgers may be strictly à la carte, but for those three, it's a bottomless buffet. Who invited them in? I look over at the door and see the hostess holding it open, even though there is no more room inside. *Great.*

We need the Headless Horseman's location before Samhain if he is to rise, the vampire says, her eyes trying to hold me hostage.

My magic may not be perfect, but vampires can't control witches. I stare back at her, flexing fists as my magic tingles faster and faster, and say, "Get out of my head." The vampire staggers back slightly, moving away. I'm so delighted, and so is my magic, which seems to pound in my hands. Someone touches my arm.

"Hey there, Sunshine."

I almost fall backward when I see who it is. "Ryan Elliott?"

My seventh-grade crush looks exactly how I remember him. His dark brown hair is slightly longer now, but he's still got the thickest lashes I've ever seen on a boy and brown eyes that suck a girl in. I've been avoiding him in school—I even had the aunts cast a spell to make sure we didn't have any classes together—but seeing him again makes me almost throw up in my mouth. Muscle memory, I suppose.

"Hey." His lips stretch in a warm smile; his eyes drop to my lips. "I was hoping to find you here. I wanted to know if you're going to Colton's party tomorrow night. If you are, maybe I could give you a ride?"

A ride? "I live two blocks from Colton's. I'm going to walk."

"What if I walked with you? We could catch up." He places a hand on my arm again. "I think about you and that night at the Gravitron all the time."

"Y-you do?" I stammer. "You mean how I bought you a POP wristband and you stood me up?" Clearly, I'm still harboring some resentment about this.

His brow furrows. "*No*, I bought you the bracelet and *you* didn't show up."

What? No. He's got this backward. I start to protest, and he holds up his hands.

"I don't want to argue. It's all in the past. We were in middle school. I will forgive you on one condition." He smiles magnanimously: "You be my date to Colton's party tomorrow night."

"Where the heck is this coming from?" I say. "You've had four years. Four years to apologize to me. To even look at me."

"I . . . I don't know," he says. "It feels like I've been looking for you forever, Katherine Hadley. And before, I was blind. But now that I can see you . . ." He reaches up and brushes a lock of hair from my forehead. "I never want to look away again."

And then he's leaning in. For a kiss? Is Ryan Elliott really trying to kiss me in the middle of this Haunted House of Hamburgers?

I rip my arm away and run, screaming, "Gotta go!"

On my way out, I barely catch Chris muttering, "Not another one."

16

Mystic Hollow Community Page

NEW POST FROM MAYOR CROFT: I am pleased to tell you power has been restored to our town. Wi-Fi issues are ongoing, but our teams are working on those as well. Halloween is saved! And now you can all post about it!

NEW COMMENT FROM FRAN CARLEIGH: Still no power at my house.

NEW COMMENT FROM ANONYMOUS: I'm not sending my kids anywhere when that flying bat with red eyes has been spotted again. What are you doing about Mothman, Mayor?

NEW COMMENT FROM RICK FAULEN: Mothman is a myth!

NEW COMMENT FROM RICK FAULEN: Okay, never mind, I saw him too.

I race all the way to Spirited Books, even though it means sprinting through the green, past the statue of Harold Croft, past what I really hope is a group of enthusiastic tourists in early Halloween costumes and not actually an entire pack of werewolves.

By the time I crash through the door, I'm breathing hard.

"Oh no," Laney says from the ladder she's perched on to restock the upper shelves. "What did Colton do this time?"

"Wasn't Colton," I gasp out.

She sighs, then steps down. "C'mon. Mom, I'll be back in twenty."

"Where going?" I wheeze.

She grips my shoulder and walks me over to Witches Brew. I've never seen it this busy—I can't tell who are students, tourists, or just plain cryptids. "We'll have our usual," Laney says, snapping at Zach.

Zach, who looks far too tired for someone who works as a purveyor of caffeine, slides two gourds over to us. "Don't snap at me."

"The customer is always right," Laney retorts.

"You two don't even pay," Zach whines as he steps away, only to return with the whipped cream canister, looping it over my cup.

I shake my head and he raises a brow, adding another spritz. Again, I shake my head. "More."

"Hadley—"

When he stops, I lean forward and press the nozzle by pushing his thumb down with my own—and then unhinge my jaw and shove my head underneath the sweet waterfall.

"That's the good stuff," I say, eyes closed in bliss.

Zach thunks the whipped cream down next to me.

"No, it's okay, I've had enough."

"That's yours now."

"Wow, such a gentleman."

"I just don't want to get shut down by the health department," he retorts, but I notice the start of a smile. "What a weirdo," he mutters as he's walking away, but I notice he keeps rubbing his thumb where I touched him.

"Him?" Laney mouths.

I shake my head. Zach? Absolutely not. We are definitely not—we've never—nothing at all.

"You're blushing," Laney points out.

"Because *Ryan Elliott* just asked me to Colton's party."

Laney gapes at me. "Excuse me, what?"

"Which should be impossible, because my sister put a love curse to make me invisible to boys—"

"WHAT!" Laney shrieks.

Oh, right. I guess I sorta didn't have time to tell her about all that, between the ghosts and the vampires and the werewolves.

"Don't worry, I yelled at her—"

"I'm not worried about *her*. I'm worried about this town! How are you going to cast a ritual with Colton if you're cursed?"

"Colton invited me to his party," I say stubbornly. "And

Harry's spell has a loophole for my true love. So maybe that's proof that he's my true love, after all. Like, if he's not impacted by Harry's spell, that means—"

"Kat?" comes a voice. "Is that you?"

I almost don't recognize Justin Tremble. Since he stopped working at Haunted House of Hamburgers, he's buzzed his hair and started wearing guyliner. Maybe he finally started that band he was always talking about.

"Justin?" My question is swallowed up by his bicep as he pulls me into a hug.

"Wow, you look so . . . grown-up," he says. "Wow. I can't believe I never noticed how gorgeous your eyes are."

Okay, this is getting weird. Still, I can't fight the butterflies. "My eyes?" I ask, sounding breathless. "They're nothing special—"

His hand lands on my jaw, hinging it back up so I'm forced to look him in the eye. "Nonsense. I could drown in those, and I'd die happy." He smiles, his thumb stroking along my neck.

I shiver, and not just because he's super-hot and he's caressing my face like he's maybe about to kiss me. For a girl who's never been kissed, it's been a strange hour. Almost makes me hopeful I'll get my first kiss this century.

This is wrong. One crush reappearing was unlikely. Two? That's downright impossible. Uncanny.

In fact, it feels like . . . magic.

"Justin," I squeak out. "Can you do something for me?"

"Anything, my love." And then he smiles, dreamily. "Sorry, that just slipped out. But I'm so glad it did. Because I do—love you."

Laney's jaw falls so far open that I have to close it manually or she's going to catch flies.

"Can you go get me some . . . more whipped cream?" I ask. When he glances in confusion at the canister, I fake a smile. "Empty, unfortunately. But I think the Stop & Shop up off the Post Road has my favorite. Do you mind?"

He reaches forward and squeezes my nose. "Oh boy," I say, his pinched fingers making me sound like a Muppet.

"Anything for my love," he says.

"Don't hurry back," I call after him.

"What was that about?" Laney asks.

"I was stalling."

"No, I mean, why is a strange college kid in love with you?"

Right. That is a little weird. I can't even remember where he went to school, but there are no colleges in Mystic Hollow. He must be home for the weekend or something. "Just proof that we need to get Colton."

"I don't know, Kat," Laney says, shaking her head. "I don't think you're *invisible* at all."

A clatter on the counter makes us turn. Zach has set down another can of whipped cream. "Heard you two," he says, like it explains anything. "Although there are twenty servings per can, so I really hope you were joking."

Oh no. Not him, too.

"Actually, we should be going."

"We?" Laney asks.

"Yes," I say grimly. "We."

I drag Laney home, but somehow Harry isn't back from her coffee date with Jack, which either means it went really badly or really—blech—well. We both spend the afternoon poring over the family spell book, but there's nothing about a love curse turning into a crush enchantment or how the town wards could turn into a creepy creature magnet or why Harry's spells to fix the house have just been breaking it more.

"It's all backward," I mutter to myself.

"Maybe Harry has the yips. Maybe all her spells are falling apart."

"Maybe," I say, but I'm not convinced.

"Why don't you try a spell," Laney suggests.

I snort. "Why, you think I can do better than Harriet Hadley?"

"Just try."

I sigh and snatch up a pad of paper. "Fine. I'm guessing you want something to eat?"

"I'd kill for a hot chocolate, actually. Someone pulled me away from my latte before I could finish it."

"Fine." I scribble down her cosmic order, then shred the paper. It's not a particularly complicated spell, so I don't need to get fancy.

Still, I'm pleasantly surprised when a cup manifests on the counter.

"Wow!" Laney enthuses. "You cast a spell, Kat!"

"You don't have to sound so surprised," I gripe.

She takes a big sip, but the next thing I know I'm being sprayed in the face.

"Ack!"

"Not hot chocolate?"

"No," she says, wiping off her tongue. "It's cold. And . . . salty. Totally the opposite of what I wanted."

I stare at her. "Say that again."

"No offense. I mean, you're still learning how to be a witch and I'm sure—"

"No, it's the opposite." My heart jumps into my throat. I cast a spell to get a sweet, hot drink and instead got a cold, salty one. Harry cast a spell to make me invisible to boys, but now I'm all they can see. "Oh no." I press a hand to my stomach, where nausea turns it over and over. Because generations of Hadley witches cast hundreds of spells to drive away all the evil. And now Mystic Hollow has become a beacon.

"Like I said," Eleanor says, floating over just as Laney takes another sip, and that's a second spit take in my face.

"Seriously?"

"Sorry," Laney whispers. "I'm just really thirsty. And I wasn't expecting a ghost in your living room."

"You should," I say, my voice low. "Because I think I reversed the wards. Mystic Hollow is about to become the most haunted place in New England."

"Well, Mayor Croft will be thrilled," Laney says in a small voice.

Eleanor frowns. "You didn't do this, Katherine Hadley."

"That's a plus," Laney says hopefully.

"You *and* your sister did this," my ghostly ancestor intones.

"Ah," Laney whispers. "Celebrated too fast."

"What do you mean?" I ask, ignoring my friend.

"I tried to warn you. The Hadley family has been the steward of magic in Mystic Hollow for centuries. You are the conduit through which it flows. But you've broken your bond with your sister, and that sacred bond is not to be taken lightly. By breaking it, you've broken the magic, too."

"What does that mean?" Laney whispers.

I gulp. "Well," I say slowly, "on the plus side, I think it means I'm not going to be single this Halloween."

A knock startles us both and Laney drops her salt water. "Don't invite in any vampires!" she calls after me, like it's a joke. But no, that's just good advice now.

Part of me expects it to be Justin Tremble with a six-pack

of whipped cream. Maybe Ryan Elliott trying to kiss me again. I even imagine it could be someone truly random, like Tom Callabra.

But nothing could have prepared me for the tousled blond curls, the one peevish dimple, and those soft pink lips.

"Reese?" I whisper.

Boys of Halloween Past

CRUSH #4: REESE WHITAKER
THE YEAR: TENTH GRADE

"Looking good, Kitty Kat," Aunt Viv says, giving my bouncy curls a playful tug as she sashays past me into the living room, wearing a glittery gold evening gown and heels too high for her own good. "Where you off to? A Halloween party?"

I look out the kitchen window at the lake in the distance. The fall foliage reflects back at me from the lake. There isn't a cloud in the sky. It is one of the warmest Halloweens I can remember, with weather in the low seventies. If I was younger, I would have loved trick-or-treating before Samhain rituals without having to wear a jacket. But Laney and I decided that this year, since we were officially in tenth grade, we were a little too old to be going door-to-door. Which frees me up to do something much better.

My favorite jeans aren't the most festive for handing out candy, but I've paired them with a black top and cute pumpkin hanging earrings. The Halloween headband in my hair hopefully is mature *and* festive. Laney and I worked hard to find me the perfect outfit because I'm going out with Reese

Whitaker, the boy I've liked all year. Someone pinch me.

I was starting to lose hope, if I'm being honest, after these past few years. After what happened with Justin—and Ashton—last year, I swore to try a Halloween without a crush.

And then I met Reese.

Well, Harry technically met Reese first, when they worked together over the summer at the town pool. But every time I'd stop by to visit, I couldn't help but stare at him in his lifeguard red swim shorts. For the whole summer, I'd get tongue-tied every time I went past him, because he was cute and he was shirtless, and when he smiled, he had this one dimple. And he smiled at me. A lot.

And then we wound up in Honors English together and everything changed.

Somehow, it was easier to talk to him about books than anything else, and Reese loved reading almost as much as me. Despite all my intentions, it happened again—a Halloween crush.

When I let slip that I think Halloween is just the most romantic holiday because it's sort of a night meant for true love in my family, Reese with his one dimple had smiled and asked me if he could come over after football practice. He even offered to meet me at Hadley Lake around four o'clock.

I watch from the window, scanning the crowd of trick-or-treaters walking around the lake for Reese. Joggers, older couples, and mothers with infants dressed as pumpkins in their strollers promenade by.

"No Reese yet, dear?" asks Aunt Diane as she comes down the back staircase into the kitchen carrying a glittery orange-and-black clutch.

"Not yet," I say, keeping my voice light. It's only 4:20 p.m. Maybe practice went late. I reach my hand into the glass jar with candy pumpkins and eat two at once. Reese never told me where we were going, just asked me if Harry would be home—I guess he wants to say hi to his old coworker before heading out. I'm hoping we'll go to the town green. Most of my class was meeting to hang out there and go to the Halloween carnival, so it'll feel like a real date if we go together. My heart swells at the idea. Me and Reese, finally. I'll have someone to hold my hand this Halloween, and maybe next year we'll be casting the ritual wards together. "He'll be here. He was really excited about it."

I watch Aunt Viv and Aunt Diane exchange a look.

"What is it?" I ask, feeling my magic tingling.

"Nothing at all, darling," says Aunt Viv. "We just want to make sure your heart is protected."

"My heart doesn't need protection," I argue. "Because he's going to take good care of it. He likes me. I'm sure, this time."

In the living room, I hear a cough. I am not even sure why Harry is still home. She's supposed to have plans with her boyfriend to go to another senior's Halloween party. This year she's dating a guy named Jack, and while I've seen Harry date a few guys, she's different around him. He even got her to dress up for the first time in years; they're wearing matching costumes and going as peanut butter and jelly. I teased her that the costumes were something a toddler would wear, but really they are super-cute. And she didn't even get embarrassed. I'm starting to wonder if Jack is Harry's person the way Dad is Mom's. My parents are out right now checking the grounds and getting ready for our Samhain rituals. We all promised to be home by eleven to be here when they perform them right before midnight.

"Reese is super-reliable. Right, Harry?" I yell into the next room. "Did he ever miss a shift at the pool?"

Harry is quiet for a moment. "Nope!" she finally says.

I look at my aunts triumphantly.

Aunt Diane gives my hand a squeeze. "He's lucky to have a chance with a Hadley as wonderful as you. And if he messes it up, Aunt Viv can turn him into a nice toaster."

"Oh, Diane! Please. The most I can do is make him eat flies. Or crave them," Aunt Viv says.

I'm not sure if she is joking.

"No one's eating flies tonight," I say calmly. "Or crow. Because he'll be here. I know he will."

With that, I turn back to the window. And I wait.

4:30 p.m. becomes 5:00 p.m., then 5:00 p.m. comes and goes. The sun starts to dip behind the trees, the grounds darkening. Our Halloween lights click on outside, and the aunts must come through and switch on a few of the lamps because I'm not sitting in total darkness, but I keep my eyes fixed on the lake.

Voices rumble from deeper in the house, my parents returning. As the evening drags on, I hear Jack and Harry talking louder and louder, and then the slam of a door, the sound of a car engine turning over. I wonder if they were arguing about who loves the other person more.

Again.

Finally, at 6:00 p.m., after no one could convince me to leave the darkened window, the doorbell rings and Laney bursts in, her Supergirl cape flapping behind her. Apparently, she decided to dress up to hand out candy.

"Kat!" She runs straight toward me and puts her hands on my shoulders as she tries to catch her breath. "Reese . . . house . . . Reese . . . house . . . Reese."

"Reese house . . . what?" I ask, alarmed, and rush her to the kitchen to get her a glass of water. "Is everyone okay?"

Laney takes a sip and looks at me, her dark eyes mournful. "I was heading to the green to stop for a pumpkin PSL at Witches Brew because this year they're making them in actual pumpkins and it's adorable and—"

"You passed Reese's house?" I fill in, trying to connect the dots.

Laney nods. "Yes."

"And?"

"It was there."

"Was he there?"

She nods again. "And . . . so was a moving truck."

I sway slightly. "No," I say. "That's not possible! Reese and I have plans. He would have told me if he was suddenly moving out of nowhere. You must have seen someone else—another van—someone else's house."

Aunt Viv and Aunt Diana seem to manifest behind Laney, their faces glum. In the doorway to the front hall, my parents appear, arms around each other. And in the far doorway, my sister leans against the jamb. She doesn't say anything, but her eyes are red and swollen. Normally she'd be here by my side already, pulling me into a hug, consoling me. Instead, she hangs back.

"Maybe someone is moving in *with* him," I suggest, panicking. "A distant cousin? A forgotten uncle? I mean, I feel like he mentioned having a step-grandfather in Arizona. And you know, it's, um, gotten really hot . . . in Arizona."

"Kat," Laney says gently, "I saw Reese walking out of his house with boxes. I saw him. They're leaving. Today. For North Carolina."

"Moving? Today?" How could Reese be so cruel? Why would he make plans if he knew he was moving? Why has no one mentioned this before? Why hasn't Reese? My hands tremble as I reach for my suddenly running nose. "Why wouldn't he tell me? We made plans. We talked about it this morning. He promised he'd be here!" I sound shrill, my throat sharp and tight.

"I know," Laney says, and her eyes are shiny with unshed tears. "I'm sorry, Kat."

"Me too," I say, and that's when I realize that I'm also crying, that there are hot tears streaming down my cheeks. I sniffle pathetically.

And then Harry is there, looking solemn as she wipes my cheeks and nose with a tissue. "He didn't deserve you, Kat," she whispers as she pulls me in tight.

I would have held her tighter, because that's the last time she hugs me. The next week, she breaks up with Jack. She throws herself into her studies. And then she leaves for BC one August morning without even saying goodbye.

17

Mystic Hollow Community Page

NEW POST FROM MYSTIC HOLLOW HOA ASSOCIATION: Former Congress Lane resident 16-year-old Reese Whitaker, who moved to North Carolina last fall, has been reported missing by his mother. She says two days ago he started talking about going to Mystic Hollow to be reunited with his lost love. She has no clue who this is. If anyone has any information, please call the local police immediately.

I slam the door in his face.

"Who was that?"

"Reese."

"Reese?" Laney shrieks. "Reese, as in the guy who moved away on Halloween and broke your heart? Reese, who completely cut off contact and ignored all your text messages? Reese, whose name you wouldn't even—" Laney cuts herself off. "Sorry. That's just super-weird, right. I mean, tell me you don't think it's super-weird."

"My sister cast a love curse to keep boys away from me, and I got into an argument with her and we accidentally broke magic, so now our town is a magnet for every evil creature who wants to eat us and all my ex-crushes are showing up, suddenly in love with me. I'd say we're well past 'weird.'"

"I said super-weird."

I blink at her.

"So what do we do?" she prompts.

"We . . ." What would Harry do? I hate that I think it, but it's all I've ever thought. For my entire life. When she started playing soccer, I waited two years and then I started playing soccer. When she did oboe in band, I waited two years and then told my parents I wanted to play oboe in band. And then Harry started going out with boy after boy, and I . . . did nothing.

But Harry has never broken magic before, and now she's MIA.

"We go to Colton's Halloween party tomorrow night," I say. "He's our only chance at fixing the wards around town."

"But will they even work?" Laney asks, her eyes huge. "I mean, if the town's magic is broken—"

"It'll work," I say. "Because it has to."

I glance over at Eleanor, waiting for her to say some convoluted metaphor about houses or sisterhood. Instead, she's silent.

"Tomorrow night," I tell Laney. "I'll meet you by the green and we'll walk over."

"Do you think there will be a green by tomorrow night?"

It turns out, there definitely is a green still. Sure, it's hard to tell who's walking over to Colton's party in a really cool costume and who is actually a ghost, but it's okay. It'll all be fine, once I get Colton to realize he's my soulmate.

"Have you seen Harry?" Laney asks nervously.

"Nope."

"Cool." She nods, making her orange wig bounce. She's going as Ziggy Stardust, David Bowie's alter ego. Laney loves his music. "And have you cast any spells that didn't immediately reverse?"

I bite my lip. The spell I tried to cast to make Aunt Diane's old jeans a little roomier have made them skintight. It's fine. I had planned to go as an eighties kid. Now I'm just an aughts kid. Right? "Not exactly—"

"We're doomed," Laney says. "Doomed—is that a mermaid?"

The girl smiling at Laney is definitely half fish, but her teeth are sharpened like a shark's. "Sort of. Keep walking." I lead her down an offshoot path, taking us the long way to the green. Plus, I can see those three vampires congregating around the monument to the first Mayor Croft in the center, and ever since Eleanor mentioned it might be tied to some witchy stuff, I don't love the idea that they're poking around it. "And we aren't doomed. You're forgetting the good news."

Colton texted me three times last night to say how he couldn't wait to see me. Just the thought makes my heart race. I'm a mix of nerves and excitement.

Laney rolls her eyes, one of which is covered in red and blue face paint shaped like a lightning bolt that goes from her forehead to her chin. The colors compliment her orange mullet wig and her wild striped pantsuit. "For once can we not talk about boys? I mean, I'm glad you're having your main character moment, but there are more important things. Like the entire town."

"I need a boy to save the town," I say. "All my life, I've been made to feel like I'm missing my better half."

Laney looks at me, her face softening so much that the painted-on lightning bolt even looks less threatening. "You aren't a half, Kat."

"Tell that to the rituals," I grumble. But still, it makes my chest feel tight to hear that. I've never had anyone tell me that. I've always been the lesser of the two Hadley sisters, the one person standing alone at Halloween with no one to hold my hand. I'm tired of feeling like the smaller half of everything.

"I bet it is sort of nice, huh," Laney muses, grabbing my hand. "Having all these boys noticing you."

I laugh despite myself. "For the first time in my life, I feel . . ."

"Enchanting?" she supplies. "Utterly charming?"

"Practically . . . magic."

Laney snorts a laugh, but then she sobers. "Oh, you're being serious. Yeah, great, Kat. You feel practically magic and there are vampires on the green."

I pull my jacket closed around me. "Yeah, that actually isn't great. Can you text your mom to maybe close up early?"

"Why—do you think they're going to eat my mom?"

I shake my head. "They aren't here because they're hungry. They're looking for the Headless Horseman's grave."

Once again, Laney bursts out laughing, then stops when she sees my face.

"There's no such thing, right?" Laney says worriedly. "I mean, I know the football team is named for him and all, but it's a town myth, isn't it? There's not really a Headless Horseman."

I'm not sure how much to tell Laney. I don't want her to freak out. I don't even know for certain myself. The Horseman is the one person my parents and aunts do not discuss. But with everything going on, I think there is reason to worry. I'll have to ask Eleanor, but I'm pretty sure the story goes that Beatrice Hadley is the one who *made* him headless. And if she did it with magic, well, with the rate at which spells are reversing, he might just be riding again soon.

"Myths come from somewhere," I say as we cross the street to Colton's.

"Okay, I texted my mom. What does yours think about the whole 'broken magic' thing?"

"Um, nothing, because I haven't really told her." I bite my lip and see Laney is about to protest. "My parents are so stressed with Grams and Grampa and being away, and my aunts are on the cruise, and they know Harry and I are fighting. I don't want to add to their worries and make them think I don't have Samhain under control. The protection spells are going to be fine," I say, trying to reassure both of us. "After tomorrow, I'm sure everything in town will return to normal."

Laney goes very pale under her Ziggy makeup. "Okay," she says slowly. "I trust you, Kat."

More kids run by and a runaway Milky Way hits my left combat boot. I pick it up and hand it to Laney, since they're her favorite. "I promise it's going to be okay. Try not to worry."

"I *am* worrying. I know you're mad at Harry, but I think you need to talk to her," Laney says as we reach Colton's house. Inside, the lights are bright and I can hear music. There are a bunch of kids hanging out on the porch. All looks normal here, at least. In the distance, a wolf howls. "If you two fighting is what broke the magic, maybe you two need to work it out to fix it."

I shiver. Laney might not be wrong. "You're right. I'll talk to her tonight. After the party." After Colton has agreed to be my ritual partner. After I know that I'm the one fixing this, not her. I'm done with being her lesser half.

"Okay, thank you," Laney says, and opens the garden

gate. We head for the front door through a tangle of bodies. Half the school must be here. Laney and I squeeze through the door where kids are holding red cups and talking. I don't see Colton, but I can hear the conversations around us, and they are not putting my mind at ease.

"I cannot get over these costumes. I swear, I thought I could put my hand through that guy's stomach!"

"And those gnomes on the counter? Have you ever seen more realistic animatronics? Those must have cost the mayor a fortune!"

"I bet the mayor doesn't know. Colton said his dad and mom have been staying at Mystic Hollow Inn for days."

"Why?"

"Who knows? Oh! Look at those animatronic bats!"

Laney and I duck as a swarm of bats flies through the house and out the back door. People laugh as if it's all in good fun, but I can feel my magic again, tingling faster and faster. I flex my fingers, try to shake them out. These aren't costumes they're talking about. Looking around, I see ghosts mingling among the living; those tiny creatures running across shelves definitely are not animatronics. They are actual gnomes. Behind me I hear a howl and wonder if someone let in an actual werewolf.

Laney grabs my arm. "Okay, those were vampires, weren't they? Any chance we can call Harry *now*?"

I am done relying on Harry. Laney wouldn't understand, being an only child, but I know I can fix this. I just can't do it alone. As I scan the party for Colton, a gnome pushes a pricey vase off Mrs. Croft's bookcase, and it shatters. A crowd has gathered around the shelves to watch them destroy the house. People raise their cups and cheer as if this is a big game.

A ghost floats through Laney's right arm and she jumps. "Seriously, Kat. Someone could get hurt. Now is not the time to be proud."

"You're right," I admit, feeling my magic tingling, my shoulders now like bricks. It's a sensation I haven't felt before, but I know something is happening, and it's all in response to what is going on here at Colton's. I need to warn him. "Let me just find Colton and tell him he has to shut this party down." I hear another crash from the other room and a girl screams. "Give me ten minutes to find him. You stay here in the open. Where it's safer."

"Are you sure about that?" Laney gripes.

"Just stay here." I race around the corner in search of Colton and instead crash right into someone tall and dark haired.

"You look like you've seen a ghost, Hadley," Zach says, steadying me with his too-big hands on my arms. It feels like I'm being smothered, in a warm and cozy kind of way. "I didn't take you for the jumpy type," he says. He's wearing a tuxedo with an eye patch, his hair slicked back. The look works for him, not that I'm about to tell him that. My stomach, however, does a strange sort of flip in response. That's new.

My smile is instant. "Are you supposed to be a Bond villain?"

"How'd you know that?" Zach asks, looking mildly impressed.

"My dad loves the movies. I've watched all of them with him," I say.

"At least you've got good taste when it comes to movies," Zach says sarcastically, and I nudge him. "Believe it or not, I brought you a peace offering. For getting us out of detention, even though you're the reason we had it in the first place."

"Agree to disagree," I say. "It was an accident."

"Uh-huh." Zach reaches in his tuxedo coat pocket and pulls out a small bag of candy pumpkins. "These are for you." A bat that is probably a vampire flitters over his head and past us, but Zach doesn't notice.

Zach bought me a present?

My stomach drops. Oh no. He's definitely another one of the boys under my sister's love-curse-turned-enchantment.

"Thanks," I say, trying not to sound as sullen as I feel.

"Don't pretend you don't love them," he says, beaming down at me.

"They're the least popular Halloween candy according to multiple surveys," I say, but my heart isn't in it.

"You aren't most people," Zach says. "And don't pretend I haven't seen you drooling over the bags we have at Witches Brew."

Despite logic, my heart flutters. "You saw that?"

Zach leans in, and it's then I realize he never let go of how he was holding me. "I always see you, Kat," he says quietly.

My heart thumps in my throat. Zach Powell is looking at me like I'm the only girl in the world. Zach Powell is stroking gently along my upper arms, his thumbs warm and soothing. Zach Powell is leaning in like he's going to kiss me, his eyes fluttering shut.

"I hate you, Harry," I mutter.

"What was that?" Zach asks, eyes snapping open.

"Nothing," I say, stamping in annoyance. It's so embarrassing that my voice comes out all strangled, because my throat is burning and my eyes are prickling.

Because this isn't real. Zach doesn't really see me. This is just my sister's spell, finding a new way to ruin my life.

"I have to find Colton."

"Colton?" Zach asks, his face falling. Then his jaw clenches. "You need to find Colton."

"Yes," I say. "And trust me, you need me to find him too. Before you do anything you'll regret."

I push my way through the crowd, trying to ignore how much it hurts. *Just a spell*, I remind myself. *It's not real, just magic*. No matter how magical it makes me feel. I'm wandering in a haze, halfway to the kitchen, when I'm side tackled. "Kat! There you are!" Colton says, bear-hugging me. And all those lonely, empty feelings vanish. Because Colton isn't just under some spell. Not when he's holding me so close. My body feels like it might burst into flames. "You look amazing." He pulls back to look at me, his eyes taking me in.

I feel slightly off-kilter like I might pass out. "Thanks." This is what I've always imagined him saying. I can't believe it's happening. Then I get pelted in the head by an avocado. "Oww!" I look up. A gnome is hurling avocados off the kitchen counter at people to much applause. Colton doesn't seem to notice.

"I'm so glad you're here," he says again, rubbing my arms. "I've been looking for you all night."

I feel my magic tingle, but my stomach is swooping at how it feels to be seen by Colton Croft. Another fruit flies past my head. *Focus, Kat!* "We need to talk. It's important." I'm talking fast, nervous now for more reasons than one.

"Then let's talk," Colton says, turning me toward the back door, leading me through the kitchen, where he gives me one of those smiles that make my whole body feel weak. "Let's go outside so we can have some privacy."

And I know I'm supposed to be shutting down this party and making up with my sister and fixing magic. But right now, it just feels so good because for once he's choosing me.

18

Mystic Hollow Community Page

NEW POST FROM ANONYMOUS: Does anyone have a number for pest control? Just found a tiny critter eating Halloween candy in my kitchen and get this—the thing is wearing a tiny hat! My husband tried to shoo it away and it bit his finger!

I've only been in Colton's backyard once before, when the mayor threw a Fourth of July party for founding families. We left early when my aunts started debating who founded Mystic Hollow—Harold Croft or Beatrice Hadley.

Colton shuts the kitchen door behind him, and the sounds of the party fade away, making my beating heart sound much louder. He isn't wearing a Halloween costume. Just his Headless Horseman jersey, but it's his party. Let him do what he wants. I don't care. I can't even think as he takes my hand and leads me over to a love seat on the porch. Even once he sits and I follow, he still holds my hand. Midnight-blue eyes, full lips, a smile I've seen in my dreams. I feel like I might spontaneously burst into flames being this close to him.

He must feel it too. This is real.

"Finally, some privacy," he says, his eyes never leaving my face. "I have been waiting for this moment all day."

"You have?" I ask. I know there was something I was supposed to tell Colton and it was important, but every thought I've ever had has just flown out of my head. "I mean, so have I."

"I know." His fingers are threaded through mine, and he's holding both my hands now.

"You do?" I whisper. My heart is pounding fast. His face inches closer to mine. Is Colton going to kiss me? This is really happening, isn't it? My stomach drops into free fall.

"I know you like me, Kat," he murmurs. "It's cute how often I catch you staring at me in class." He gives a small laugh. "You looked so mad the other day when I was talking to Zara in chemistry."

My face flames. I guess he noticed that.

"So what is it you like about me?"

I hide an awkward laugh. "You're, um, really cute."

He smiles.

"Is that so?"

I nod.

"What's your favorite feature?" He leans in, and when I laugh again, he nuzzles me, and the feeling of his nose in my hair sends heat down my spine. "I'm serious. What makes you like me, Kat? It's been months and you stare at me all day. What are you looking at?"

"I don't know," I reply, my voice going high and embarrassed. "You."

"Me," he replies, then starts humming. "You impressed that I'm the mayor's son?"

"Mm-hmm," I reply, although it suddenly feels like it takes effort to keep smiling.

"And that I'm our QB? Did you know that no one else in the tristate has my completion percentage?" Okay . . .

"And did you see how many followers I have? Wait—let me show you. I have this hilarious video, and it's going viral—"

He fishes in his pocket for his phone and starts showing me "just one more video" about how great he is. And yes, I've seen all of them, but it's different when he's the one showing me, pointing out how "huge" his shoulders look or the "sick" swoop in his hair.

By the time we've gotten to the fifth video, I realize he hasn't asked me a single question that wasn't about him. And I haven't spoken in . . . a really long time.

I had been hoping that Colton Croft loved me back, but I'm starting to wonder if Colton just loves . . . Colton.

"Ask me a question," I blurt out as Colton switches from his videos to his photos. He almost drops the phone in surprise.

"What?"

"A question. Ask me. Anything."

He thinks for a moment, and then his eyes light up. "Oh, I've got one."

"Yeah?"

He leans in with a smile. "Yeah. Can I kiss you?"

He closes his eyes and puckers up and just waits. For *me* to kiss him. He's got to be kidding me! I'm about to tell him to shove it, when I hear a strange sucking noise.

My magic tingles again as if it wants attention. *Danger. Danger. Danger,* it seems to say. I pull my hands away from Colton. "Do you hear that?"

"I only hear you," he says, eyes still closed. "I only ever see you. I only ever want to feel you."

Did I really think this guy could be my soulmate? Maybe Harry is right.

I almost groan aloud. Of course. Colton is just another victim of the Harry Hadley Love Curse Reversed. But then I hear that suction noise again and turn to the backyard. A shadowy figure leans over a body on the ground. Vampire. My blood runs cold and it all comes rushing out: how this party needs to end, how much danger we're in, and how I really, really need Harry's help. "You need to get inside," I whisper, pulling Colton up to standing. "Right now. And tell everyone to go home. You have to stop the party. It's not safe."

Colton blinks confused. "Not safe? What do you—?"

I know I'm not making sense, but Colton is under my

spell, literally. I could say anything and he'd still love me, right? It's sort of a superpower, one that I plan to use to save the day. "Because I want you to," I say quickly. "I'm worried everyone is going to get partied out before my party tomorrow. So send them all home. Right now." I push him toward the back door and practically toss him inside. "Hurry!"

Thankfully, that seems to work. Colton looks plenty upset and rushes back to the party.

There's no time to waste. I whip out my phone (promising myself I'll unfollow Colton the second I'm not trying to save the town) and click on the flashlight.

It illuminates Tom Callabra, motionless on the ground. One of the vampire girls leans over him, a swirly straw stuck in his arm. As I gape, her cheeks hollow out with another sickening suction sound. Tom may be a jerk, but he doesn't deserve to be sipped like a smoothie.

"Back away from him!" I yell, rushing at them. I can feel my blood pulsing through my veins as I keep one hand out in front of me as if I know how to stun the girl by sheer will with my magic. "Vampires aren't allowed in Mystic Hollow! You're breaking the rules of Hadley magic."

She sits back and laughs as she wipes a drizzle of blood away from her bright red lips. "I'm breaking Hadley magic?" She laughs cruelly. "You already did that, you little witch. Didn't you know your powers come from your bonds? Or did your little coven forget to teach you that?"

"I know it now," I mutter. "But just because Mystic Hollow has turned into a magnet for the supernatural thanks to your spells reversing, you don't *have* to kill my friends."

"Relax." The vampire prods Tom with the toe of her high heel and he groans, his head lolling. "He's not dead. And I'm certainly not here because of any spell you cast. I'm here for the Horseman, because me and my sisters can finally step on this hallowed ground."

"You want to lay flowers on his grave or something? Because I can call my mom and ask where it is—"

"Where it is, where it was," the vampire says with a smirk. "Because tomorrow night, now that the wards are no longer keeping us out, he will rise from his grave. And finally complete what your ancestor so foolishly tried to stop by beheading him."

"Oh," I say as I subtly kick the straw out of Tom's inner elbow. "And what was this bucket list? Wordle streak? Try every flavor of Airheads? Visit every pumpkin patch—?"

"World domination," the vampire interrupts, flashing her fangs. "Too long we have been forced to live in the shadows. When the Horseman returns, he will make sure that we walk in the light."

"You're a vampire," I point out, gently kicking Tom aside. He rolls a bit away, which probably won't feel great when he wakes up, but I just need him away from her. "Are you sure sunshine is your thing?"

She snarls again. "I will be grateful when the Horseman

rises and finally silences you and your friends. Mystic Hollow will become a realm for the undead—everyone else will die." She grins at me, all her pointy teeth on display. "Happy Halloween, witch."

And then with a flick of her wrist, she transforms into a bat and flies off into the night.

19

Mystic Hollow Community Page

NEW POST FROM DAVE LEYLAND: Avoid Hadley Lake! I repeat: Avoid Hadley Lake! I was walking my dog around it this afternoon when a giant tentacle came out of the water and pulled a deer into the lake! I sound crazy, but I know what I saw.

The wind seems to carry me home. I rush past the town green filled with people enjoying Mystic Hollow and feel a pit in my stomach when I think about the werewolves, Mothman, and vampires here with them. And now the supernatural want to help resurrect the Headless Horseman so he can turn Mystic Hollow into a realm for the undead? Clearly that myth is not a myth. He's as real as all the other supernatural beings who are showing up. Between that thought and all the running, I'm hyperventilating as I reach the house.

"Harry!" I scream. "Harry! Vampires are in Mystic Hollow! Where are you?" I'm racing down the hall toward the kitchen when the rug is pulled out from under my feet. Literally. I hit the floor with a thud. Tiny figures in pointy hats, one wearing a string of pearls, another carrying Aunt Viv's favorite brooch, run past me. "Gnomes! Who let them in?" I scramble to stand, and Phoebe drops from a table above me, all the fur on her back spiking up, hissing at the garden gnomes. Suddenly one of the gnomes staggers backward, clutching a candy bar.

And then it's raining candy. I look over to find Harry, pelting them with candy.

"They like the chocolates best," she says as the gnomes giggle and race off with their treasure.

"Harry," I say, but now that we have time to talk, I'm not sure what to say. "I—I think I need to say . . ."

"I'm sorry," she says. "It's all gotten way out of control."

"I just watched a vampire drink a football player with a straw," I say, and Harry's eyes widen even more. "And that's not all. I'm seeing ghosts everywhere, and I think there is a werewolf hanging out at Witches Brew."

"The kitchen has turned into an ice realm," Harry blurts out.

"How?" I screech.

Harry nods, swallowing hard. "I was halfway through the cookies 'n' cream—" She cuts herself off, reddening.

"So I take it the conversation with Jack didn't go well?"

She hangs her head. "Um, no."

I push open the door to the kitchen, tensing up at the blast of arctic air. "You weren't kidding!" I dart inside, ducking icicles from the ceiling, and grab the pint, yanking two spoons from the gnomes snacking on the counter. I offer her one. "Whatever happened with you two? I mean, I feel like you disappeared senior year, and then you were broken up, and you were in college."

Harry slumps down onto the floor, weakly reaching out with her spoon. "Witchcraft 101. Spells take intention . . . and sacrifice."

I sit down next to her, hard. "Do you mean . . ."

"To stop you from breaking your heart, I had to break mine." She digs into the ice cream. "I sacrificed our relationship. Erased his memories of us, of me."

I'm too stunned to even eat ice cream. She stares at me innocently over a huge bite of cookies 'n' cream.

"And you just went to talk to him?" I ask.

"Mm-hmm," she replies through a full mouth. When she swallows, she adds, "I had to lure him to that coffee shop with a long story about my lost dog and when I got there . . . his eyes just slipped over me. He didn't recognize me. Of course he didn't. I couldn't handle it."

My spoon clatters to the table. I can't believe my sister went through all that. Sure, I'm pissed at her, but no one should have to go through that. "Harry," I try, my voice low, but she waves me off.

"I kept telling myself the fate of our town depended on

me making him fall in love with me all over again, but I couldn't even go over and introduce myself. I followed him around, trying to get the nerve . . . but I couldn't do it." She sighs, her ice cream forgotten as my stomach churns. When I reach for her hand, to, I don't know, let her know that I'm here, she pulls away. I watch as she fixes a smile on her face. It's as flimsy as a mask, but I can tell she needs to change the subject or she'll cry. "So how was your day?"

"Oh," I say, trying to sound breezy, "I just threatened some vampires who say they want to bring the Headless Horseman back to life so he can continue his reign of terror over the living and kill everyone in Mystic Hollow or something. All they need is the location of his grave and then it's game over for all of us living folks, I guess."

Her face pales. "They said that?" I nod. "This is really bad. The Horseman's grave is under Hadley House. If the foundation keeps cracking, they're going to be able to raise him."

I feel a chill that sweeps through my bones, and I'm not even sure where to start. "What are you talking about? He's real? Like really real?"

Harry looks frightened now too. "Yes. It's a secret Hadleys have kept since Beatrice, well, you know." She drags her hand across her throat. "I found a whole entry about what happened in the family spell book. He's kind of the whole reason we do the yearly protection spells." She rubs her face with her hands. "The magic here keeps him contained, but now that the house is breaking . . . Kat, the veil between the supernatural and Mystic Hollow is falling. Samhain is tomorrow. And neither of us have anyone to do the rituals with. We have to call Mom and Dad. Or at least the aunts."

"Okay," I say slowly. "Okay, let's just think about this. You have no one who loves you." Harry groans and throws her head back. "And I have dozens of boys professing their love for me. Surely we can work something out."

"It's so stupid," Harry gripes. "We're witches. Why do we need boyfriends to do magic?"

Despite it all, I almost laugh. For once, Harry sounds like the sister I grew up with.

We're interrupted by a strange moan from the kitchen. The two of us look at each other, then slowly push open the swinging door. That's when we see the sink. It's filled with slushy water, and a green tentacle is muscling its way out of the drain. We both scream.

"What is that?" Harry freaks out.

"Kraken." Eleanor appears through the nearest wall to join us. "There's one in the lake behind the homestead that Hadley magic has kept contained. At least, it did."

I bolt for the switch next to the sink and flick on the garbage disposal. There is a tiny scream, a funnel appearing in the water before it turns to chum. I fight the urge to throw up.

Eleanor floats over, glancing down at the dirty water with

distaste. "Wonderful job, Katherine, but remember, that's just a tiny tentacle. The real thing is in the lake." She glances our way. "If you don't deal with the true problem at hand, creatures like that will keep appearing all over town."

"What does that mean?" I ask. "We're calling in the aunts. They'll cast the spell with their husbands."

Eleanor, however, sighs. "A spell. Wonderful idea. How have those been working out lately?"

My stomach tightens as I look at Harry. Didn't we just have our sister moment?

"I believe forgiveness is the foundation of a healthy relationship," Eleanor adds.

Forgive her? I feel bad that she dumped her boyfriend, but she cursed me to remain loveless. And then stopped talking to me.

"Eleanor is right," Harry says quietly. "I need to try to forgive you. If you apologize, I think I can."

20

Mystic Hollow Community Page

NEW POST FROM ANONYMOUS: Just saw a kid howling at the moon. What is happening?

The silence in the kitchen is deafening.

"Whenever you're ready," Harry whispers as Eleanor watches us.

But I'm too stunned. My magic is tingling softly, and I can't decide if I'm more angry or hurt. "Apologize to *you*?" I rear back at her. "You cursed me! Literally! All these years, every time a guy ignored me or dated someone else or laughed at me when I asked him to dance—it was all your fault! Did you think it was funny, parading around here with all your perfect boyfriends while I was heartbroken and alone?"

"I wasn't *parading*," Harry says back, breaking off to sneeze three times in a row. Around us, the house shakes. "And every single Halloween, every single other day of my life, I've dropped everything to try to help you. I even gave up the love of my life! I've always just been trying to protect you. What else was I supposed to do? I'm your big sister. It's my *job*. And you think it was easy, setting a good example for you? Getting good grades. Never breaking any rules. Getting all of Mom and Dad's attention and obsession—all the rules they gave me that you managed to shrug off. You have no idea how hard it was. I've had to do everything first, by myself."

"You weren't by yourself!" I roar back. "I was by myself, because you cursed me to be!" I toss aside my spoon—it hits a gnome in the head and it grumbles something, but I don't care. "You want to know what it's like to be by yourself? Fine."

Then I turn and run.

"Kat! Wait!" Harry calls, but I only run faster.

The leaves crunch under my feet, and I'm unsure where I'm going. All I know is that I don't want to be anywhere near my sister. So I keep running, headed toward the green, my lungs and legs burning.

It all comes rushing back, every Halloween being brokenhearted.

Ryan ditching me at the Gravitron in seventh grade. Hunter turning me down at the dance in eighth grade. Justin never getting my note at Haunted House of Hamburgers. And worst of all, Reese moving away.

Wait a minute. If she cast the spell last year, when she and Jack broke up, the only one affected would have been Reese, right?

And if that's true, what happened with Ryan, Hunter, and Justin?

Is Laney still at Colton's house? Did she go home? I reach into my pocket to try to call her and realize too late I left my phone at the house. I ran off in such a hurry, I don't even have a coat, and now that I've stopped moving, I'm shivering. And then I remember what she said, that I always make things about boys.

She's right, and maybe Harry's right too.

Every Halloween, I've made it about my crush. I can't think of a Halloween in years that I just spent with Harry or with Laney or even with my aunts or parents.

I wrap my arms around myself and try to crunch into a ball. I can smell the fried dough from the Halloween carnival and wish I'd brought my wallet. Drowning my sorrows in powdered sugar feels right. "Great. Just great!" I yell at the clouds keeping the moon from showing itself.

"Hadley?" Zach walks toward me, his tuxedo jacket slung over his shoulder. The white shirt shows off the broadness of his shoulders and chest I've never noticed before. He flicks his eye patch up to look at me with both eyes. "What are you doing out here? Colton said the party was over but said it was because you wanted them to save their energy for your party, which he told everyone they had to go to, by the way." I fight the urge to swear aloud. "But that can't be true, because I know you, and that's not the Kat Hadley that I know."

He removes the eye patch, then reaches into his pocket and pulls out his glasses. It feels like something settles when he slips them onto his face, like I had missed him looking like himself. *Zach looks good in glasses*, I think, and feel the strangest sensation of butterflies in my stomach.

But it's just Harry's spell. Zach doesn't "know" me. He doesn't "see" me. This is just some big cosmic joke. "You don't know me at all," I tell him, rubbing my arms to keep warm. "I did want him to end his party so that everyone would come to mine. And now I don't even want to throw the party. I'm selfish and obsessed with boys liking me, but no one likes me, not even my sister, and I'm pretty sure I deserve it."

"I like you," Zach says, his eyes all big and puppy dog.

I shove at his absurdly broad chest. Seriously, he's supposed to be a nerd. Is this just part of the spell too? "No, you don't. That's just the spell talking."

He clears his throat. "Um, you do look like you left home in a hurry. Where is your coat?" He doesn't give me time to answer. "Take mine," he says, handing me the tuxedo jacket.

I'm too tired to protest. I slide my arms into the jacket, which is still warm. The sleeves are too long, but I like it, curling my fingers inside as my magic seems to hum in Zach's presence. A small, mean part of my mind tells me that the real Zach would never give me his coat. The real Zach would get all competitive, tease me for forgetting mine, talk about how his brothers love him so much more than my sister loves me.

But maybe I need this Zach, right now.

"Do you want to talk about it?" Zach asks, putting his hands in his pockets. "I'm a good listener. I never get time to talk at my house with my brothers always trying to dominate the conversation."

"I know a little about that myself," I admit, thinking of my competitive streak with Harry. Zach waits for me to say more. At first, I want to stay silent, but then I realize: This is a spell. I can say anything and Zach won't leave. After that, it's much easier to open up. "My sister thought she was helping me with something, but really, what she did hurt me. And I'm not sure how to forgive her, even though we're sort of up against a deadline with Samhain—I mean Halloween—tomorrow."

"Halloween." Zach nods. If he thought Samhain was a weird word, he isn't letting on. "And this Halloween deadline . . . you have something important to do . . . with your sister, right? And maybe it has to do with all these weirdos we've had in town?"

I'm pretty sure Zach knows I'm a witch. I hold my breath, not daring to speak. Instead, I just nod.

"And you don't want to work together with her because you're mad?"

"I can't," I say, unsure of how much I can share. "It . . . it won't work if I'm mad at her."

Instead, he just nods, running a hand through his hair,

and I watch the action as if it's happening in slow motion. Zach really does have good hair. Ugh! What is with me? This has to be Harry's spell! "I know I don't know what you're mad about, but this sort of fight happens with my brothers and me sometimes." He looks at me intently. "I get mad. They get mad. That's normal. But the important thing is to realize that relationships are all about sacrifice. It's not even. It's not always intentional. But being someone's family, loving them, you have to give up that selfish part of yourself. You have to learn that it's bigger than just you. Love, connection, sacrifice—it's the foundation. And you can't build yourself up on your own, just like you can't build a house without a strong foundation."

This time when my magic tingles, I know what it's telling me. Zach is right. (As much as it pains me to admit, he's actually really smart.) This is what Eleanor meant.

I have to find a way to forgive Harry, and she has to find a way to forgive me. And then we'll call the aunts or Mom and Dad, and someone will cast the rituals, and we'll save the town and maybe also the world.

"Sorry, does that make sense?" Zach asks with a cute little laugh.

"Weirdly, it sort of does." I can't forgive Harry for what she did, but a part of me does understand she was trying to help me, and maybe that's a kind of forgiveness. And it explains why she's been so distant. "Listen closely, Powell, because I'm not going to repeat this, but you're pretty good at this advice thing."

Zach's face brightens like a sunrise. "I know I am. That is also why I'll be valedictorian next year."

"I think you're pronouncing *salutatorian* wrong," I tell him and feel some strange need to reach out and touch him. A poke, an arm squeeze. *Something.* I don't let myself. Instead, we both just stand there awkwardly staring at one another again, the sounds of kids on the Tilt-A-Whirl at the carnival carrying on the wind.

"Want me to walk you home?" Zach says suddenly, and again my stomach feels like it's on fire. "Or are you planning on fleeing into the night and howling at the moon?" He cocks his head to the side. "I hear there's a werewolf on the loose."

He doesn't know the half of it.

Even if I don't want to hash things out with Harry, I don't have a choice. Samhain is tomorrow. We have to fix magic now. "Sure," I say, feeling slightly nervous and unsure why. *Harry's spell*, I tell myself.

We turn in the direction of my house and walk quietly side by side for a few minutes, the only sound the dead leaves beneath our feet. The wind sweeps through my hair, blowing it in front of my eyes, and I bump into Zach as I try to get my bearings. He reaches out a hand to steady me.

"So when Colton shut down the party tonight, he told

the entire school they *had* to come or his dad would banish everyone from town, although I don't remember those mayoral rights in the town charter," Zach says, giving me a lopsided grin. "So I guess you can't be mad that your mortal enemy is there, since it was mandated."

Crap. This is bad. I cannot have the entire school over to my house right now! There's an ice realm in the kitchen and gnomes on the piano, not to mention the fact that the house might be crumbling away to reveal the grave of the Headless Horseman, just in time for him to end his centuries-long nap. "I'm not having a party. It's . . . not a good idea right now." Is it me or does Zach look disappointed? "But if I was having one," I say quickly, "I'd want you to come. If you promised to not do Mr. Ruth's extra-credit assignment so I could get a few points higher than you."

"You wish!" he says. "Okay, well, if anything changes, just know the Powell boys would come. I can even take my Bond villain costume out for another spin. My dad won't need his tux back till his company black-tie event in December, and I think it would be cool celebrating Halloween—I mean, Samhain—with you."

He used the holiday's correct name! His cheeks go all ruddy and it makes my stomach flip-flop. And then a wolf howls, far too close for comfort.

"We should both get home," I say hastily, pulling my arms out of his tuxedo jacket and reluctantly handing it back to him. I'm a few houses from home. Hopefully Harry will be waiting.

He rocks back on his heels. "Telling me what to do, Hadley?"

"Yes," I say. Now I know what I need to say to Harry. "Yes, I am."

21

Mystic Hollow Community Page

NEW POST FROM MAYOR CROFT: It has come to my attention my son has been telling people to go home and save their Halloween spirit for tomorrow. This is untrue. Please proceed with your regular Halloween preparations. We want tourists to remember this Halloween in Mystic Hollow forever!

I don't have to look hard to find Harry. When I walk up to the house, she's waiting on the porch, wearing an oversize black knit sweater of Mom's. Behind her, the candles in the house are flickering like there's a poltergeist inside. I wouldn't be surprised if there was at this point.

"Hey," she says quietly, and I watch her face crumble. She wipes away a tear under her left eye. "You forgot your phone and I was getting worried. I think we should talk."

Why is she the one crying? She's the one who cast the spell. "I don't want to talk to you." I walk past her, then whirl around. "Actually, that's not true." I let the porch door slam shut. "Harry, you cast a spell on me without telling me, and then you expect an apology? I didn't make you erase your boyfriend, and I know you loved him, but I was in love, too, or, like, close to being in love. With a really great guy. Or maybe you don't remember Reese? I get that the other guys weren't into me and weren't nice, but *Reese*? You worked with him. He was even really close with you too. You were, like, best friends!"

Harry sets her jaw. "We were."

I stare at her. "Is that all you have to say?"

She stands up and pulls me inside the house. "Look, I'm sorry, okay? Do you forgive me? We need to just forgive each other and move on so we can save the town."

As we walk back through the entryway, I don't even recognize our family home. Garden gnomes sprout between the floorboards like weeds. The house is cold and seems to breathe, creaking and groaning and—is that a growl?

Harry only stops once we're standing over the crack that cuts the house exactly in half.

"Just apologize, and then we'll call the aunts," she says, sweeping her frizzy hair behind her shoulders with that classic perfect Harry composure.

I grit my teeth. I can't believe I have to apologize to her for anything considering what she did to me, but I know that the magic needs us to repair our bond, so I try to summon any genuine regret I feel. "Fine, whatever. I'm sorry. I'm sorry I've been so boy crazy and so boy obsessed. I'm sorry

I turned Halloween into something it's not."

Harry nods. "I forgive you." She glances down at the crack as if expecting it to have healed itself. Instead, a gnome flings a banana peel at her head. It sticks. I watch her curl her lip in disgust.

"Okay," I say, rolling my eyes. "Well, we apologized. We've probably fixed magic or whatever."

I wait for Eleanor to float by and tell me how wrong I am, but for once she's strangely silent.

"And the wards?"

"Tomorrow night, I'll cast them. Alone."

"Alone? That's not how it works!" Harry starts to say.

"We're witches, Harry. We don't need *boyfriends* to be magical. If your backward spell has taught me anything, it's that I'm magic. On my *own*," I say, more confidently than I feel. "And another thing, my party is back on." Harry starts to protest. I don't need to tell her it sort of wasn't my idea. "They'll be safer here and you know it."

Harry sighs deeply. "You might not be wrong about that. And fine. I'll do the spell, too."

I continue, feeling a fire in my belly. "Perfect. You can go to the cemetery to do the protection spell at Beatrice's grave while I do the protection rituals here at the house. We'll see who's the stronger witch, once and for all."

"I don't know if this is the best idea," Eleanor interjects, finally manifesting behind the couch.

"Stay out of it, Eleanor!" we both snap, and then I feel

bad when I see the look of hurt on her face. She disappears in a flash. Harry and I stare each other down. I wonder if we're both secretly thinking the same thing—that we're not at all sure that doing the spell separately will work, but there's no way we're going back now.

"I think this is better for both of us," I declare, willing myself to believe the words. "This way we don't have to have anything to do with each other."

"Great! Sounds like a plan," Harry says icily.

"*My* plan," I remind her, and then we turn in separate directions, going to our own sides of the house. Even without the crack, this home has really split in two, because our sisterly bond, or whatever was left of it, is officially severed.

22

Mystic Hollow Community Page

NEW POST FROM MAYOR CROFT: Happy Halloween! Don't forget to post your videos with #mystichollowisthebest!

"And then I said, 'The party is back on! I am not doing the rituals with you! You do some and I do some and after that, I don't want anything to do with you,'" I tell Laney. "I haven't seen her yet today, but I think she's been gathering her own materials for the ritual."

"Well, I'm glad she isn't coming to your party," Laney says with a sniff. "I can't believe she cast a spell to make you invisible to boys. Tonight is going to be epic."

"As long as the world doesn't end."

"Which you won't let it."

I nod. Usually I'd be so excited to be having everyone over to my house. I sent a party evite out to the grade right after my fight with Harry. Colton was the first one to RSVP. Ryan said yes as well and so did Hunter. It looks like there are tons of people coming, which I keep reminding myself is a *good* thing. I won't invite any vampires in. There has to be some Hadley magic still working in this house. And then I can keep an eye on all my classmates, duck all the magically lovesick crushes from my past, and make sure the Headless Horseman doesn't rise.

Piece of cake.

At least Laney and I don't have to waste time with decorations. This house already looks haunted with torn wallpaper and cracks in the walls. Laney came over early to help me clean up the best we can and put away any witchcraft items I don't want out at the party, even though I do need some for the spells later. We're also trying hard to keep the garden gnomes outside, but it's an uphill battle.

"There's something I don't get though," Laney says, yelling over the ABBA album she put on for cleaning. "If Harry confessed about the spell and you both apologized, why is the house still falling apart?"

"I don't get it either," I admit. I look over at the nearest wall. The cracks have splintered, snaking in every direction. Plus, as an added bonus, green goo is oozing out of them too. I can't shake my uneasiness. Is this party a good idea or a bad idea? Am I wrong about casting the rituals separately? Mom did say the spells have to be cast by "hearts that beat as one" or whatever. I shove another handful of candy pumpkins into my mouth. "But it's definitely her fault. This whole thing is her fault. Which is why, as far as I'm concerned, I don't even have a sister anymore."

The house rumbles. Laney and I jump as a crack carves along the floor.

"You don't think the house is going to fall down around us, do you?" she asks. "Maybe we should have the party outside." She looks out the window at the lake and swallows a scream as one of the kraken's tentacles pulls a deer under the murky water. "What was that?"

"A kraken," I say, starting to panic that Laney might be right. But outside is no better. The garden gnomes have taken over all the flower beds, uprooting my mother's favorite lilies and growling at the squirrels.

"Kat!" Laney protests. "I take it back. People are not safer at the Hadley House. This is the gateway to hell. There's a portal to the ice realm in the kitchen. A kraken in your lake. The only place that's safe is the greenhouse!"

"Actually, that's off-limits too," I say, gnawing on my lip. "Victor, our Venus flytrap, seems to have grown five times his size overnight. I'm worried he might have acquired a taste for something bigger than flies."

Laney drops her feather duster and stares at me. "OMG. You're keeping Audrey from *Little Shop of Horrors* in your greenhouse?"

This is one Broadway connection I don't think my aunts would appreciate. "It's going to be okay. I put up signs."

When I gesture at the "Danger, Keep Out" that I handwrote on printer paper and taped up in the kitchen, greenhouse, and by the lake, Laney's frown only deepens. "Everyone is still safer here at the house than they are walking around Mystic Hollow. It's better if we keep everyone close. Colton texted me he's telling everyone he knows to be here. He's texted me a ton today, actually. He said he can't wait to see me again tonight."

"Yeah?" Laney asks.

I sigh deeply. "And it's all because of the spell, isn't it?"

She gives me a sad smile, then pulls me in for a hug. "I'm sorry, Kat. This really sucks."

"That's not the worst part," I mutter into her shoulder, as she squishes me closer. "I don't even think I like him anymore."

As we do our best to mop the walls—they've started bleeding now, which is mixing with the green goo for a truly appalling sludge—I fill her in on how Colton only wanted to talk about himself and how he was so in love with himself.

"That might be the only thing you have in common," Laney says with a small smile. "You both love Colton Croft."

I flick some goo at her. "Yeah, right." I sigh. "It's not like I can expect to find a guy who actually has things in common with me. Like, who would that be?"

Laney gives me a look. "Yeah," she says sarcastically. "It's not like there's one guy who's been literally trying to do all the same things you do, all the time. Who challenges you to be the best version of yourself *and* gives you free coffee."

My cheeks burn. For some reason, I don't want to tell Laney that Zach has fallen to the love spell, too.

Because does that mean that I secretly had a crush on him this whole time?

I look at Great-Aunt Aida's portrait for answers, and I swear, if she had laser eyes, she would have hit me with them by now. The hand in her portrait has moved as well, and she's now pointing directly at us, which doesn't feel like a good sign.

"Can I say something to you without you getting mad?" Laney asks. Her nose is running and her breath appears as she talks. I'm not sure if the temperature is still dropping from the ice realm or it's from Eleanor appearing behind her.

"You're my best friend. You can say anything," I tell her.

"I'm happy you finally have some boys paying attention to you. Even if it's just a spell. Really. And you are the smartest, most hardworking person I know, but all this," she says, looking around at the crumbling house, "is a lot without also having to perform magic tonight. Are you sure you're up to doing this alone?"

To be honest, the closer it gets to sundown and the rituals, the more nervous I feel. Mom and Dad texted me and Harry this morning reminding us about what herbs to gather, where to place the sigil, what spells to say and when. Harry and I answered separately. The first spell has to be done at moonrise, then the other right before midnight. She raided the dried hydrangeas from the greenhouse, which are the first thing we need to burn, and I'm pretty sure all the ceremonial tapers are missing from our mantel. No matter how mad I am at Harry, the thought of doing this alone still makes me sad. It's fine, though. There are more hydrangeas in the garden, and I'm pretty sure we have a pack of birthday candles in the junk drawer.

I try to put on a brave face for Laney. "I'm going to be fine. We're almost done cleaning, so I have plenty of time to gather ingredients for the spell. We've got plenty of time."

There's a growl in the kitchen, followed by a crash, and Laney and I jump.

"That does not sound like a garden gnome," Laney whispers.

"It's not," Eleanor says. "A creature has entered the ice realm in the kitchen. White. Large. Furry. Lots of teeth. He does not seem to be enticed by the candy bars like those gnomes are."

Laney and I look at one another. "Yeti."

"But it's fine," Laney says, glaring at me, "because you put a handwritten sign on the door."

I frown at her. "Should I have printed it out? Would Comic Sans help this situation?" The doorbell rings. "That must be the first of the trick-or-treaters."

"This is so exciting!" Eleanor exclaims. We both turn to look at her in surprise. "What?" she asks, looking embarrassed. "I died before this holiday really became something *fun*. A day where everyone celebrates witches. How grand!"

"Just don't scare anyone," Laney says, giving Eleanor a sideways look.

"Like I could," Eleanor says with a grin. "They'll just assume I'm part of the decorations!"

She isn't wrong, unfortunately.

I open the door and find a grown man. Laney and I relax a smidgeon. At least Eleanor won't scare an adult. Plus, he might get a kick out of her clothing; he looks like he's part of a historical reenactment.

"Greetings," he says, sweeping the pilgrim hat from his head in a flourish-filled bow. "I seem to have lost my way. Pray tell, which is the road to the great colony of Roanoke?"

"He's dead," Eleanor whispers from behind me. "He might not realize it."

I try to give him my best smile, but when I look him in the eye, I can see the oak tree *through* him, and that still makes me a little queasy. "Just a moment." As covertly as I can, I pull out my phone. Will Google have directions to a sixteenth-century colony? As I'm busy checking the directions—better switch to walking because I doubt this guy has Lyft—Laney nudges me. "Twelve o'clock," she murmurs.

I look down our drive to see Justin Tremble returning. He's carrying four bags on each arm.

"Hey," I say weakly as Justin bounds up the steps, the bags swinging. "What are you doing here?"

He grins. "I heard you were throwing a party. And since

you mentioned you liked whipped cream, I bought every can I could find. In a three-hour radius." He leans against the doorframe with the sort of smile that says he thinks this is totally normal and looks at the pilgrim. "Hey. Cool costume, dude."

"Good tidings," says the pilgrim with a nod.

My heart is beating fast. One thing at a time, right? That's how I study for exams, handle my homework. I'm not first in my class—or, at worst, second—for nothing. I turn to the pilgrim. "So you are way too far north. What you want to do is head south and keep going on foot for the next . . ."—I scroll through the directions and gulp—"twenty-two days."

The pilgrim, however, looks undeterred. "Thank you. Fare thee well," he tells us both, and turns to go. After consulting the sun, he turns and strides directly into the forest.

Justin frowns. "Is he actually walking?"

"Method acting," I say quickly, and my rambling explanation is cut off by a loud roar from the kitchen. The door shakes. Justin doesn't seem to notice. He's just staring at me with a goofy expression.

"So," Justin continues, "when does your Halloween party start? I can help you set up. Let me put these in the kitchen—"

"No!" Laney and I cry at the same time. I drag him away from the door. So apparently those Do Not Enter signs are not as effective as I was hoping. "We were, um, just cleaning the living room. Maybe you can help Laney finish."

Laney gives me a look. "Why doesn't he help *Kat* finish?"

I lean in to her and whisper, "I need to gather ingredients for the spell. Harry took everything from our stores." She gapes at me. "But don't worry. I got this. You just . . . keep him in the living room, okay? Don't let anything eat him."

Laney glares at me. "Fine. But you owe me."

"Thanks," I say, ducking out into the garden. My mom has some hydrangeas over by the fence. She's already picked all the pink ones for the spell since they represent romantic love—but these flowers change color based on the acidity of the soil, so there are only blue ones left, and they've been fading with the frost.

I try to remember what I read in my witchcraft books. *Blue hydrangeas: Apology. Regret. Forgiveness.*

Well, that'll have to do. I'm not exactly feeling in a *romantic* mood. I bat my way through the overgrowth of sunflowers, grumbling to myself.

"Hey there, Sunshine," comes a voice.

I almost scream and fall back, but Ryan Elliott has an arm around me. "Ryan! What are you doing here?"

"I was thinking about you," he says. Okay, creepy. "And I wanted to bring you some flowers."

"You decided to pick them from my garden?"

He reaches up, and after some huffing and puffing, rips the big stem down the middle. We're well past flowering time, so the sunflower is reduced to seeds, all the petals gone, but he doesn't seem to notice. "A sunflower for my Sunshine."

I try to offer him a smile, but it feels more like a grimace. "How nice of you." I rack my mind trying to think of a chore to give him, but he's probably safer at the house. "Do me a favor?"

"Anything," he says, smiling at me in that vacant, besotted way. He's trying to stuff the sunflower behind my ear, but it's far too big, and the leaves are scratchy along my temple.

"Help Laney get ready for the party? We have some cleaning—"

Ryan grins. "I'd love to. Since we're hosting together."

"Sure," I say, pointing him toward the living room. Laney is going to kill me.

The next thing I need for the spell is rope we can knot and bury—I've been practicing the intertwined overhand knots before I could even make bunny ears on my sneakers. Harry took the ritual rope we use, which was braided out of our ancestors' hair (gross, but powerful), so I go to the greenhouse to find some twine that my dad used on the tomatoes last season. It'll do.

And last, an apple. The two lovers usually each take a bite, sealing the ritual. It's some metaphor for temptation. Maybe I can send Ryan to the Stop & Shop or ask Colton to bring one over? Because I am not risking the kitchen, not when I hazard a glance in the window and see that the yeti appears to be juggling garden gnomes. They're not too upset, at least, so maybe it's some kind of game.

Yetis are famous for their playful spirits, right?

In the end, I decide it's too dangerous to send any boys anywhere. I grab my reusable bag, yell to Laney that I'll be back in twenty, and throw open the door . . . on a line of boys.

These aren't just my crushes. This is every guy at Mystic Hollow High. They're lined up one behind the other, each one waving to me. A few have flowers in their hands. One has balloons. When I step out onto the porch in shock, one breaks from the pack and jogs up the front stairs.

"Hey, Kat," says Reese, his eyes like saucers as he stares at me. "I thought I'd come early to help you get ready for the party."

"So did I," says Hunter, and offers me a bouquet of fall blooms. "What do you need help with?" He flexes a muscle. "I can lift anything you need moved for the crowd."

My face flushes. For just a moment, I feel like I'm having the best dream of my life. A nervous giggle escapes my lips before I can contain it. "I . . ." I struggle to find actual words. They stand there waiting. "I'm . . ."

"Hey, guys? I've got it covered," says Justin, coming up from behind me and stepping out onto the porch. Next thing I know, Ryan reappears too. The four of them immediately start arguing. Over me. I can't believe what's going on here. I need to stop this. More boys are joining in on the porch now too, trying to get to me and the front door. And then Laney jumps into action.

"I've got this!" she says, pushing past me. Her eyes find mine. "You find that apple and then we start casting the rituals. I'm not waiting for moonrise."

I'm not sure what she says to them, but it must be about me and some sort of competition, because the long line of boys follows her into the house, flexing and puffing their chests and standing up as tall as possible. I shut the door behind them, breathing hard.

But there's one more boy on my porch.

"Hadley," says Zach, holding up a sack that is swinging, growling coming from inside. "What the heck did you do?"

23

Mystic Hollow Community Page

NEW POST FROM ANONYMOUS: Has anyone else run into a guy dressed as a pilgrim asking for directions to Roanoke?

Laney will be fine. She works at a preschool in the summer months and has to deal with toddlers all day. These guys will be a piece of cake. And they'll all be safe inside our house.

"What is going on in there?" Zach asks suspiciously, looking around at the house in shambles. Eleanor has thankfully disappeared. The bag in his hand swings as he looks around; the growls only grow more violent. I don't have time to stand and chat. Thankfully, Zach follows as I stride down our driveway. There's a market on the green, which isn't too far of a walk. Hopefully they have some apples.

"Just some early party guests," I say, trying to compose myself. Spell malfunction or not, I'm going to let the sight of all those boys clamoring for my attention live rent-free in my mind forever. When we reach the street, Zach brushes a low-hanging tree branch out of the way for me, and I try to ignore the way it makes my heart flutter. "What do you have in the bag?"

Zach holds the bag out of reach. "Found this thing trying to tear Witches Brew's coffee stash apart about an hour ago. Am I right to think this thing belongs to you?" As he leans in toward me, my heart jumps into my throat. Because my heart doesn't know this isn't real.

"Let me see," I say, reaching for the bag.

"Don't let it out," he warns too late. I peer inside and am greeted by a green scaly face. That's the last thing I see before I'm knocked on my butt.

Is that a *gremlin*? It races down the path to the town green, scaling a tree and dive-bombing into a jack-o'-lantern. The pumpkin turns to mush, but thankfully there are about a thousand along the green. The mayor really went all out this year.

"But for the record, that creature is not mine," I say, breathing hard.

Zach offers me a hand, and I take it so he can lug me to standing. He quirks one eyebrow and looks at me over his glasses. "Where are we going?" Zach asks, sounding mildly concerned.

"I need an apple," I say, choosing honesty. I'm tired of lying, and he's under my spell, isn't he?

"Must be a serious craving if you're leaving your fan club at your house." Zach walks beside me down the main path of the green, skirting the statue of Harold Croft with a frown.

"It's for a very special family . . . recipe," I say. "One that I need to . . . make tonight. At moonrise."

"Sounds like a very special recipe," Zach agrees. "Can I help?"

I glance up in surprise. The bell on the door tinkles as we step into the little market. "Yeah, um, just find an apple, okay?"

"Fresh out," comes a voice, and the grocer is standing there, hands on his hips. "*Someone* posted that Mystic Hollow's apples are 'hashtag the best.'" Five guesses who that was. "Tourists came and totally cleared us out."

"Wait!" Zach crows, racing over to a far corner. "Found one!" He holds it up triumphantly, like it isn't bruised and battered and dusty from rolling across the floor.

"We'll take it," I say quickly, opening my wallet.

Zach pockets it, his coat bulging, and we head back the way we came.

He nudges into me with his body, walking into me a bit. "Early mystery guests, some family recipe involving apples . . . I have to say, I'm getting pretty excited for this party."

I bite my lip. "You sure you want to come? I mean, really, you, Zach Powell."

"Yes, I, Zach Powell," he says, chuckling a bit.

I grab him by the arms and stare deeply into his eyes. "But do you really?"

He laughs but doesn't lean away. Suddenly I realize his hand is brushing a curl out of my face, tucking it behind my ear so gently I can barely breathe. "Yes, Kat. I really want to go to your party."

It's probably safest if he comes.

"But you need to stay out of the kitchen and the greenhouse," I say.

"Drat. That's the only reason I was coming."

"And don't go anywhere near the lake. There is a kraken." The words roll off my tongue with ease. I've never been this open about anything supernatural with anyone outside our family other than Laney. I've certainly never talked to a boy about witchcraft. Zach, though, is different. We've always watched each other closely, following each other's grades, activities, and debated over extra-credit points. Something tells me Zach can handle this information.

Zach nods and puts his hands in his pockets and nods like I'm merely discussing the weather. "Got it. Lake, off-limits unless I bring my cutlass."

"And my bedroom—"

Zach stills, his smiling fading. "Let me guess. Monster under the bed?"

I shake my head, my cheeks pinking. "I . . . no," I say, shaking my head. "I always thought that before I'd have a boy over, I'd clean up the stuffed animals. And I was going to invite . . . someone up there tonight."

"Colton," Zach says, his face falling. He draws in a slow breath. "What makes you think he wouldn't want to see your stuffed animals?"

I shake my head. "It's childish. What boy would think that's okay?"

"I'm a boy and I think that's more than okay," Zach says with a smile, and it breaks my heart, because it's that same besotted smile every other love-spelled boy has been giving me. "Although I don't think it's okay you wanted to hide them."

That surprises me. "Why?"

"Any guy who likes you should like all of you, Kat. Stuffed animals and all."

As we step up onto my porch, the wood creaking, I can feel my cheeks flushing more. For some reason, I want nothing more than to introduce Zach to all my stuffed animals by name. I bet he'd say hello to each and every one of them.

"What does your sister think of you liking Colton?" Zach asks as I go for the doorknob.

I drop my hand. "Harry? I don't know," I say, and feel strange talking about Colton with Zach. "I haven't really asked her. She doesn't get to decide who I like."

"I know. I just meant because she was so upset about what happened with Reese Whitaker. I figured . . ."

I snort. "She wasn't upset that he moved. She seemed weirdly thrilled."

"No." Zach pulls the apple out of his pocket and tosses it in the air, eyes fixed on it as it spins. "I mean when he kissed her."

24

Mystic Hollow Community Page
NEW POST FROM ROB KERCHER: Did anyone see that thing fly over the green? It had red eyes. Is it safe to be trick-or-treating right now?
NEW COMMENT FROM HAYLEY DRUTHER: I saw it too! There are also green scaly creatures attacking Witches Brew. Steer clear!

Colton told everyone to show up at seven, and by seven fifteen the house is bursting at the seams, people packed like sardines in every room of the first floor. Even so, the doorbell keeps ringing, groups of people showing up, many I don't even know. While I was gone, Laney convinced my group of admirers to start a game of flag football—apparently whoever wins, wins my heart or something—so they're busy in the front yard while Laney and I control the door, making sure we don't allow any vampires inside. Zach and his brothers are on garden gnome duty. I'm not sure what Zach told his brothers, but they don't seem alarmed to find living, evil garden decorations running though my house. All around me, people are dancing, laughing, and having fun, not realizing my house is falling down around them. I try to focus, but all I can think about is Harry.

Zach says they kissed, my sister and *Reese*, but she was dating Jack. Why didn't she tell me?

"Great party, Kat!" someone yells.

"Slime on the walls! So cool, Kat!" I hear someone else shout.

"Where'd you'd get the animatronic gnomes, Kat? Colton had these too!" a third person asks me.

I try to smile and be in the moment, but Harry is all I can think about. First she stole all the supplies for the ritual, and now she's gone, hopefully to the cemetery—since my mother always said it was the other most magical spot in Mystic Hollow. Does she know that I got my own ingredients? Has she started casting yet? And is she still thinking about Reese? Suddenly I wish I could talk to her.

The doorbell rings again and Laney opens it. Two Confederate soldiers walk in side by side and join the fray.

"Cool costumes!" Justin says to them, then turns to me with the look of a lovesick puppy. "I feel like you're avoiding me. Can we go someplace and talk?"

"Kat! Over here!" A guy I don't know is waving wildly to me from the dining room, where he's standing on one of the chairs.

"Hey, Kat! You look amazing tonight!" another guy yells, even though I'm pretty sure I have slime in my hair.

I'd love to think all these guys want to talk to me because I'm so magnetic, but I know Harry's love spell is on the fritz and clearly things are getting worse. Somewhere in the house, I hear a wolf howl over the sounds of Taylor Swift.

Laney looks at me and mouths, "Are you okay?"

Not really, I want to tell her. I wish I had time to fill her in on everything, but there are too many people. My watch alarm goes off, reminding me it's almost time for the first spell—I glance out the window to see the full moon, looking far too large through the branches of the willow tree. And the doorbell rings again. Laney opens it.

"Hi! Hi! Hello! Hi there!" I recognize the guy right away. He's cleaner than the last time I saw him, and his extensive facial hair has been tamed. He takes one look at Laney and breaks into a wide grin. "Girl! It's you! Bookstore girl! Love you!" He grabs her hand and pulls her toward him, practically lifting her into his arms.

Laney squeals as he puts her down. He's still holding her tight. "Hi. I'm Laney."

"Laney!" he repeats, and spins her around. "Love you! Treats?"

And now I'm certain. Mystic Hollow might have had werewolves, but now we have a were-boy. Unfortunately, he used to be Zach's and Laney's joint-custody stray dog named Ronald/Fred. Should I tell her the truth? "Um, Laney?"

"You came as Wolverine," Laney is saying to him as she ignores me. "I love that character. Let me show you where the treats are in the other room." She looks over at me shyly and mouths, "He's cute," as he drags her away, chanting, "Treats! Treats! Treats!"

I think she'll be okay. After all, she wanted a golden retriever boyfriend. Right?

"Catch!"

I duck barely in time to miss a garden gnome flying just overhead. A gremlin comes from out of nowhere and grabs it, and they begin wrestling in time to the music. The guys just laugh. "Look at that thing! What is it?"

Okay. I definitely need to cast these wards. And they have to work.

My phone buzzes. It's Mom on the family text chain.

Mom:

Everyone ready? We miss you both but know you'll do great.

Dad:

Don't forget to wear your hats and send us pictures. It's tradition!

The hat! I almost forgot. I rush back into the dining room and go to the armoire to pull out the hatbox with our cartoonishly large witches' hats stacked inside. Harry's and mine are both here. I feel a strange pang when I realize Harry has left without hers. She's a stickler for tradition and, like Mom, she would never do Samhain without it. Something is wrong. I can feel it. But then my phone alarm goes off again, and I know there is no time to second-guess myself. The first spell has to be cast.

I head to the back of the house with the hats to where my parents' office is. I've hidden my supplies in their locked room, which leads to a side door. The first spell is a simple one. I just need to burn some flowers.

"I can't believe I'm doing this alone," I say to myself. Sure, this is what I wanted. I told Harry to work separately. I wanted to send my aunts on a cruise. I was excited Mom and Dad would be away so I could have this party. But now, as I am about to do a Samhain spell alone, I realize I miss them.

It doesn't matter that I've got a whole town full of boys, all clamoring for my attention.

"I'm here," Eleanor says, and immediately I feel cold at the base of my neck.

I spin around and see her standing in the doorway. I wish I could hug her. "You're back!"

"You and all your gentlemen callers looked as if you needed some privacy." She gives me a stern look. "Though that many suitors calling on one lady would have been a scandal in my day."

"I know," I say, oddly cheered up at the sight of a ghostly relative. "Do you want to do the first part of the spell with me?"

Eleanor smiles sadly. "You miss Harry, don't you?"

"How'd you know that?" I ask.

"I can just tell. Harriet had the same look when she left the house earlier. You two are lucky to have each other." She wrings her hands. "I wish I still had my sister to talk to."

"What happened to her?" I ask. "With the two of you, I mean?"

"We had a terrible row right before I fell ill," she says. "It's so long ago, I don't remember who was at fault, or what the argument was about, but when she came to see me to make amends, I pretended to slumber so she left. Then I died before we could speak." For once, Eleanor doesn't look smug or in control—she looks devastated.

"Oh, Eleanor!" I gasp. "Is this why you haven't moved on? I'm sure your sister would want to see you. You're being too hard on yourself."

Eleanor's lip trembles. "But what if you're wrong? What if she's still cross with me?"

"She's not," I insist. "Sisters forgive each other." I stop short, realizing what I just said.

Eleanor doesn't seem to notice. She absentmindedly pulls a candy bar from her pocket and takes a bite. "I wish I remembered our row. Maybe I've been wrong all this time and my sister really did have my best interests at heart."

Like Harry, I realize.

The clock in my parents' office chimes. It's 8:00 p.m. Time for the first spell. *Please let this work, even though I'm alone*, I pray, suddenly overtaken with terror that I'm about to ruin everything.

"You better hurry," Eleanor says, forcing me out of my spiral. "I'll stand here with you the whole time."

I pull all the spell supplies out of the cabinet and cram my hat on my head, leaving Harry's in the box. Eleanor nods encouragingly as I step outside and walk down the back steps. I look around for gnomes, but there are none, so I pull out the supplies.

Will fresh flowers even burn?

"Focus on your intentions."

I inhale slowly, lighting the birthday candle. Its flame is weak and small, but that shouldn't matter. My intentions are big.

Protect my friends. Protect my family. Protect my home.

I hold the blue petals to the flame, but all I can see in my mind's eye is Harry's face. *I don't have a sister anymore.*

"Focus!" Eleanor reminds me.

I bite my lip. Right.

Cast out the creatures who would do us harm. Protect this town. And don't let the Headless Horseman rise out of his grave and try to eat us all.

The flowers flare to life and I gasp as the fire consumes them, the tingles in my hands growing into something more—something that feels like power.

I stare at Eleanor in surprise.

"Did I just do it?" I ask, my voice catching.

Eleanor doesn't look elated. Instead, her eyes are wide in panic. "Kat," she says. "What did you do?"

"The protection ritual!" I say, but my heart is suddenly beating in my throat far too fast. "To keep us safe. To keep the Headless Horseman from—"

But my words are swallowed up as the ground begins to shake violently both inside and outside the house. Eleanor and I look at one another in a panic as everything around us starts to sway. I rush inside with her and see the books in my parents' office falling from shelves, the lamp tumbling off the table and crashing. Garden gnomes pop up from holes in the baseboards and cracks in the wall and scatter, screaming their little heads off as they run full tilt. Then there is an ear-piercing crack that sounds like lightning, and a gaping hole appears in the middle of the office floor.

25

Mystic Hollow Community Page

NEW POST FROM ANONYMOUS: Anyone got the details on the silent rave happening at Mystic Hollow cemetery? Lots of people wearing glow-in-the-dark costumes. But no music?

Smoke rises from the hole in the floor, obscuring my view, but I don't need to see to know what's down there.

"What in the blazes is that?" Eleanor panics. "You don't think . . . it can't be . . . is it . . . ?"

"The Headless Horseman's grave opening?" I whisper, my heart pounding hard. "Yeah, I think it is." Because I cast a spell to close it.

And magic is still backward. I've just unearthed the monster who wants to end my town.

"What about the rituals?" Eleanor exclaims, her eyes wide as saucers. "Your sister—you must try again!"

"I know! I know!" I say, standing at the edge. "How did

Beatrice send him to the grave the first time?"

"She beheaded him!" Eleanor snaps. "But something tells me that won't work this time!"

"Thanks for the reminder," I say, starting to sweat. I need to do something. Normally I have all the answers. To calculus. AP Language essay questions. But right now, faced with an undead Headless Horseman rising and wreaking havoc on Mystic Hollow, I have no clue what to do. I'm in a full-blown panic. And then my phone starts to ring. I pick up without looking. "Harry?" I say, hoping.

"Kat?" Aunt Diane's voice is on the line.

"Oh, Aunt Diane! Thank the stars," I blurt out, my panic obvious. "You have no idea what just happened. The house started shaking and then a hole appeared in the office and—"

"*Katherine*," Aunt Viv cuts in. "What just happened? Something is really wrong with the family magic. Your aunt and I can feel it all the way across the ocean. My knee has been killing me so much I lost at shuffleboard. Explain!"

"I think Harry and I accidentally opened the tomb of the Headless Horseman," I say fast, and wait for her to start yelling. "Or I did. I'm not sure."

"What?!" Aunt Viv squawks.

"We broke Mystic Hollow's magic, because Harry cast a curse on me, and I wouldn't apologize—"

"Katherine," Aunt Diane says, her voice low and deadly.

"You need to finish the ritual with Peter. Right now."

"I know," I whisper, my stomach tightening. "But who builds a house over an ancient cemetery where the Horseman is buried?"

"Witches!" Aunt Viv says defiantly. "Who better to keep him down where he belongs than the coven that put him there?"

"I guess you've got a point," I agree.

"Listen to us, Kat," Aunt Viv finally says, her voice eerily calm. "You have to close the grave at once."

"I lied about having a boyfriend. I don't have anyone to do the rest of the ritual with me. The handfasting, the apple biting . . . how am I going to do it on my own?"

Aunt Diane swears under her breath.

"I just wish the rest of you were here to help us," I say, my voice going whiny and pathetic. "I shouldn't have sent you away." The music in the other room grows louder. "I shouldn't have cared about some stupid boy and having a party. I wanted to do it on my own, with some boy, but what really matters is family."

"What's done is done. Focus on the now," Aunt Diane says sternly. "We're going to open a portal and come help you. Stand back."

I watch, fascinated, as my aunts begin chanting a spell I've never heard. My phone heats up slowly, and then all at once, until it's almost too hot to hold. But I grip it tightly, hope even more painful. They're using my phone to make a portal.

But as quickly as the warming begins, the phone grows cold again.

"The Bermuda Triangle!" Aunt Viv cries in frustration.

"It's not that, Vivy," Aunt Diane says. "Kat told us. The magic is broken. It's too dangerous for us to portal. We don't know where we could end up." She turns back to the phone. "We will try another way, but you can't wait for us. You need to redo the ritual. Start over! Remember: love that burns, love that binds, love that finds. You need the flowers, the rope, and the apple. You have to stop the Horseman before he raises his undead army—"

"His what?"

"The Horseman. He controls the dead. When he rises, he will raise every soul in Mystic Hollow, and they will join him as his army to kill every—"

The line goes dead. I look at Eleanor in a panic. There are lots of things in Mystic Hollow in my direct path that want to eat, bite, and maim me and the citizens of Mystic Hollow, but I need to get to Harry. I don't care about the rituals. The Headless Horseman has risen and is about to raise all the dead. And my sister is alone in the cemetery. "I have to get to Harry but someone has to watch the house."

"You can't," Eleanor says. "That's foolishness. You need to complete the wards—"

"I need to get to my sister," I yell as I race out the door.

One step, and my feet go sliding out from under me. I've stepped in green slime. I scream as I start to fall. Hands reach out to grab me.

"I've got you!"

I look up in surprise. Colton cradles me in his arms while looking down at me adoringly. "Hey, you. Cute hat."

I touch my head and remember that I've gone fully witch. "Yeah. Hey," I say, confused when I look around and see the party is still in full swing. "Didn't you feel the earthquake?"

"The only earthquake I felt was the beating of our two hearts as one," Colton coos, smiling goofily. "You can't believe I'm saying this to you right now, right?" Colton goes on. "I get it. Average Kat Hadley going out with Colton Croft? It sounds impossible, but here I am."

I brush him off. I can't stand the idea of him touching me another second. "I'm flattered, but, um, could we talk about this later? I have to find my sister."

"You don't need your sister. You have me." He grabs my hand and leads me through the foyer, pushing past people to get outside to the porch, not stopping till we reach the side of the house where it's quieter.

Almost too quiet. All my senses heighten.

Twinkle lights dance in the wind, except I didn't put up any decorations—those are will-o'-the-wisps in the lake, trying to draw people to their death. Nearby, the greenhouse is glowing with a strange pulsing green light. It would be super-romantic, except I'm pretty sure the world is ending, and I'm with a boy I don't even like. "Colton, I really have to go."

"Whoa. What's your rush? The party is a hit thanks to me. I kind of told everyone I was your cohost tonight. Everyone wants to go to a party with Colton Croft, you know?"

And now he's talking about himself in the third person. A few days ago, the thrill of being this close to Colton would have made my stomach flutter, but now all I can think about is my sister. I see a flash of light and look up at a window.

Our house looks like it's having a fit. The lights are flashing yellow and green. A group of gremlins clamber down the drainpipe. Garden gnomes shatter the windows and scuttle their way inside. The window to the kitchen has iced over. The wind shifts again, and leaves blow in our direction, bringing along with it an icy cold that reminds me of the one rising from the hole in the office. Something is happening. We're being watched. I pull on Colton's hand. "We aren't safe out here, Colton. We need to get you inside."

"You're with me," he says, puffing out his chest. "Where could you be safer?"

That's when a horse's whinny cuts through the air.

I look around wildly and pull on Colton's hand again.

"Kat—"

"Shhh!" I hush Colton, but he doesn't listen. He just keeps talking about himself and how happy I should be that he noticed me and how I don't need my sister or anyone else, and that's when I see a tall figure emerge from the shadows behind Colton.

I'm too late. The Headless Horseman has risen from his grave.

I'm so petrified, I can't even speak. I tug on Colton's arm to pull him away, but I'm too late. The Horseman kicks his horse into a gallop, and they're looming closer and closer. He raises his gloved hand, and I watch in stunned disbelief as his axe falls.

26

Mystic Hollow Community Page

NEW POST FROM MAYOR CROFT: Citizens, I've been alerted by numerous reports of small critters on carnival rides, eating wires, and causing havoc at the festival. Please avoid the area for the time being while we deal with this minor issue. Tricksters at work, I'm sure!

A scream builds in my throat as Colton's head rolls to a stop in front of me, his eyes blinking in surprise. The Horseman continues down past the lake, loping toward the cemetery, but I can't look away from Colton's disembodied head. As if feeling left out, his body ambles over and casually picks up his head, which he holds like a football tucked under his elbow. I guess he is a quarterback.

"Cool, how'd you do that?" his head asks, laughing hard, not at all concerned. "Neat trick. I have to show the guys." He jogs back toward the house, carrying his head.

I whirl around, but the Horseman has already disappeared

into the woods. The cemetery is on the other side of the lake, and I need to find a shortcut. Fast. It's not like I can run quicker than a horse.

"Wait! Stop!" I scream.

I hear someone snicker. When I turn around, I see a group of vampires.

"You're too late, witch," says the one who bit Tom. She wipes a dribble of blood from her mouth, and I pale thinking of whose that could be. "The Horseman has risen from your prison and now will raise the dead to assemble his army." She steps closer, and I can feel the darkness in her trying to swallow my energy whole. "By midnight, the veil will completely fall, and then Mystic Hollow will be ours."

I picture the town green, where everyone is gathered for Halloween. The carnival blazing bright in the night, the pumpkin patches, haunted corn maze, and the trick-or-treaters. These supernatural beings our family have kept away for centuries will be allowed to run free and will take over our town. I can't let that happen.

The vampires start coming at me, baring their fangs.

I know they're expecting me to panic, but I refuse to be afraid. I'm a witch. My family vowed to protect this town centuries ago, and somehow I lost sight of what these Samhain spells are for. They're not about finding love on Halloween. They're about coming together as a family to protect Mystic Hollow. But it's not midnight yet. There are still two Hadleys in this town, and together we can save Mystic Hollow.

Instead, I turn and race toward the little rowboat we keep by the edge of the lake. Yes, there's a kraken. Yes, there are lights in the water trying to lure me to my death.

But my sister is across this lake, scared and alone in a cemetery, and the Headless Horseman is riding there to raise his undead army. I get into the boat.

The vampires hiss and lunge at me, but a tentacle rises out of the water and bats them aside like bowling pins. They topple as I start rowing.

On the far shore, tombstones seem to bob with every stroke of the oars.

While not a Samhain ritual, per se, Mom has always brought us to the cemetery on the holiday to visit the graves of our ancestors to thank them for all they did to protect Mystic Hollow. There are many Hadleys buried here, but Beatrice was always our first stop because the woman was a rock star witch.

While our house holds more power, it makes sense for Harry to try to cast her spells there.

I jump off the boat, not bothering to tie it up, and race through the cemetery, trying painfully hard to ignore the blue orbs everywhere and the eerie low-lying fog as I reach the oldest part of the cemetery, next to the church. There's the sound of hoofbeats in the distance, and I know the Horseman isn't far behind.

I whirl around, looking for his dark form, when I crash into another body.

Harry. When we crash together, she drops what she's carrying—charred remains of hydrangeas, a nub of a candle, our family ceremonial rope, and a bushel of apples.

"Harry!" I throw myself at her for a tackling hug. "I'm so glad you're all right."

Harry falls to her side, me on top of her, and looks up in surprise. "Kat? Oh my God. I'm so glad *you're* all right."

We hold each other tight, and I think we're both shedding tears.

"I tried doing the first spell on my own like you wanted, but I don't think it worked," she tells me. "As soon as I finished, there was an earthquake, and the graves are shifting. I—I think I might have raised the dead, Kat. I failed. You must hate me."

"Oh, Harry, I don't hate you," I say, sniffling. "You're my sister. I love you. That's why I was so mad about the love spell. Why didn't you just tell me Reese kissed you?"

Harry's eyes widen in surprise, and she pushes her frizzy hair out of her face. "You know about that?" I nod. "I felt so awful. I didn't know how to tell you. I knew how much you liked Reese, and right before Halloween he kissed me. I didn't want to kiss him! I pushed him away immediately, I swear. And I told him I never wanted to see him again. But then he started flirting with *you*, and I knew he was just doing it to get closer to me. And . . . I didn't want him to hurt you. You'd been hurt so many times before with the others! That's why I cast the spell—to protect you." Her lower lip trembles. "I had no idea the spell was powerful enough to make Reese's family move *right then.* When that happened and you were so upset, I knew I couldn't tell you the truth. I was so mortified and I felt so guilty, I guess I pulled away so you wouldn't know what I did."

This all makes so much sense now. "I thought you shut me out because of something I did," I confess, a lump forming in my throat. "I thought maybe you stopped talking to me because I couldn't live up to be the perfect Harriet Hadley's sister—that I was pathetic. That—that I couldn't even get a boyfriend."

Harry looks shocked. "Is that what you really thought?"

"Well, yeah," I admit. "You're so good at everything. Spells. School. Life. Boys. You cast a large shadow. There's just no competing with you and, believe me, I've tried."

"Oh, Kat!" Harry hugs me again. "That wasn't it at all! I was ashamed about what happened. You were right—I was trying to control your love life, and I am anything but perfect." She wipes her nose. "Far from it. College is nothing like I thought it would be. I built my whole high school years around winning. Then I got into Boston College like I always wanted and everyone is smart there. *Everyone* does well. And now I don't even know what I want anymore." She cries harder. "And to top it off, I think my roommate hates me. I haven't made any real friends yet, so I just spend most of my time in my room talking to my parents on FaceTime. I'm the pathetic one."

I squeeze her hand. I feel terrible. "Oh, Harry! Why didn't you say something? You're always telling Mom and Dad on the family call how BC is amazing."

"I was so embarrassed," she says. "My friends from home are all loving life at their colleges and don't have time to talk. You and I weren't really talking. I've just felt so lonely."

"So have I," I admit. "I know I have Laney, but you're my sister. We've always been so close, and then when we weren't, I was so mad. I'm sorry. I should have never let boys come between us."

"I'm sorry too," Harry says. "I wish you could forgive me."

"Harry," I say, smiling a bit through my tears, "you're my sister. I know you acted out of love, and you made sacrifices too. Of course I forgive you."

There's a clap of thunder, and the sky washes with lightning.

"What was that?" Harry asks, just as a metallic screech cuts the air. The cemetery gate is opening.

"The Headless Horseman. You know how you think you raised the dead? I raised the Headless Horseman."

"Oh my," Harry says, watching as his black horse paces down the cemetery path. "What do we do?"

My sister holds tight to me, and she's asking *me* what to do.

"We try again," I say. "Together."

She looks at me in surprise, and I reach for the closest flowers I can find—plastic daisies someone left on a grave.

"The ritual," I say. "You and me."

"You need your true love," Harry says, staring in horror as the Horseman approaches, raising his axe in threat.

"I love you, Harry," I say. "And that's true."

She strikes a match and holds it to the plastic flowers. They aren't hydrangeas. They aren't even real flowers. But I know my love for my sister is strong.

"Protect this town," we both whisper. And then we hold our breath, wondering if the flowers will catch.

"Kat," she whispers as the Horseman approaches, his axe glinting in the moonlight. "I want you to know, I love you—"

"Don't," I whisper back as the ground underneath us fractures. Green and gray hands shoot up, clawing at the earth. The Horseman's army is rising. "I love you too, Harry."

And then I shut my eyes.

Heat flares in my hands, there's a ghostly whinny, and then a rush of wind.

When I crack my eyes open, the Horseman is gone.

"Did it work?" I ask.

"It's just the first part of the ritual," Harry says, squealing a bit as a hand reaches for her ankle. Because now we have zombies. "We need to finish it."

I paw along the ground, trying to grab the rope and the apples, as an entire woman's torso rises out of the earth, her eyes milky and unfocused, her hands reaching for me. Harry screams and hauls me back. "Leave it!"

"But we need the objects."

Harry hauls me away from the cemetery, dodging zombies as we go. They groan at us, and Harry screams right back in their faces, a feral noise. That's my sister. "We need to send the Horseman back to his final resting place. Just like Beatrice did."

"We can't behead him again."

"I'm sure she used a spell. We just have to find her spell book. Mom mentioned she had more supplies in the office—"

"The green!" I say, pulling at my sister's arm, tugging her in the other direction. "Eleanor said they buried her spell book in the monument at the center of the green. We get that—we get new supplies for the ritual—and we finish this!"

In the distance, we hear screams and that all-too-familiar call of the Horseman's steed.

"We banished him into Eastbrook," Harry whispers.

"Well, by the sounds of it, he's headed back here. Let's go!"

And with that, my sister and I take off running together toward the green.

27

Mystic Hollow Community Page

NEW POST FROM CLIFF PARTON: I thought the Headless Horseman was supposed to stick to the parade route. Why is he riding past by my house on a skeleton horse holding a sword? New routes should always be cleared with the HOA first!

"Run!" Harry cries, but I stay calm and grab her hand.

I hold tight to my sister's hand, feeling like I'm five again as we run out onto a deserted street. Carnival lights flicker in the distance, pointing us to the green—and the spell book we need. Trick-or-treaters are in for the night, thankfully, since every supernatural being I can think of is on the loose, but the green will be packed. Far too many people for the Horseman to hurt. And if he kills them, they'll join his army of undead.

We don't need any more zombies.

"What's still open in town?" Harry asks.

"The market is out of apples," I tell her. "And for rope, we can try the hardware—"

I glance over to see Zach in front of Witches Brew, waving at me.

I race over.

I see Zach eyeing my hat with amusement. "Um, why aren't you at your party?" He holds the broom under his chin and rests his head on it. I'm just happy to see he still has one. "My brothers are still there, but I left after a bit." He looks at me pointedly. "You seemed sort of busy. With Colton."

"Oh." My stomach drops and I feel a flutter in my belly as Zach stares at me. "We were just talking about his head," I say, and he looks at me quizzically. "I mean. I . . . we . . . aren't together. I don't want to be together," I clarify. "I'm just hoping his head will be back together with his body soon."

"O-kay," Zach says slowly, trying to follow.

Harry clears her throat and looks at us both. "Hey, Zach," she says.

"Hey, Harry," he says with a nod.

"We need to borrow a few things," Harry tells him. "It's urgent."

"Right! Yes, urgent!" I say, looking around and trying to compose myself. I brush past Zach into the café. To Harry, I say, "Maybe a cake pop?"

"Those have apple in them?"

Zach walks over. "This for your recipe?"

I grab him, one hand on either side of his face. "Zach, I'm going to say this once. It's not a recipe. It's a spell. I'm a witch. The Headless Horseman is coming, and we need an apple to stop him."

He stares at me. "Darn it. I was really hoping you were making some amazing apple pie." He easily vaults over the counter, which he probably has done a million times, while Harry rolls her eyes and steps behind it by walking around. "What about apple cider donuts?"

"Zach Powell, I could kiss you," I say, snatching the baked good from him.

"And the rope?" Harry reminds me.

Zach whips off his apron, extending it by the ties. "You can knot this."

Well, it'll have to work.

"Oh! And do you have a hammer?" Harry asks him.

"We need a hammer?" I ask, confused. I don't remember a hammer being in any of the spells.

"For the monument," Harry says, looking at me.

"Right!" I turn to Zach. "We also need a hammer."

"O-kay," Zach says slowly. "We've got a toolbox in the storage closet." He points and I race over. "Should I ask what's going on?"

"No," Harry and I say in unison as we go running from the café.

I double back, just a few steps. "Stay inside, okay? The

Horseman is coming with his undead army, and I'm pretty sure he's going to try to kill us before we can send him back to his grave."

Zach's brow furrow worriedly, then it relaxes. "Let me know if you need another donut."

I laugh. "That's all you have to say? You're not at all worried?"

"You're the smartest person I know," Zach tells me, the corner of his mouth lifting into a smile. "I'm sure you can handle it."

I shake my head in amazement. "How come you understand me in a way no one else does?"

Zach stares at me seriously. "Because I know you."

I hear Harry calling from the monument, holding a rectangular shape aloft. Beatrice's spell book. She's found it.

"Zach?" My stomach flutters as he looks over at me again. "Am I really the smartest person you know?"

"Well, yeah," he says, blushing slightly. "You keep me on my toes, Hadley. And I know I give you a hard time about stuff, but you make me better at everything."

I think about Zach, my sometimes cranky, competitive lab partner and academic rival who brings me candy pumpkins, doesn't care that I have stuffed animals, and likes me just as I am. Maybe I have had a crush on him this whole time.

If only his feelings for me were real and not just a spell.

"I wish I could kiss you right now," I say without thinking.

"What did you just say?" Zach says in surprise, and steps closer.

Another scream cuts the air, and I turn to see the Headless Horseman approaching. This time, he's flanked with his undead army. As he nears the pumpkin display, he bends from the saddle and scoops one up, affixing it to his shoulders. The jack-o'-lantern flickers back at me.

Why did he have to pick one that was carved to look like the poop emoji?

"Oh, shit," I whisper. The church clock tower chimes. It's midnight. The veil is falling. We need to stop the Horseman *now.* "Zach, I gotta go."

"I'm not leaving you," Zach says gruffly, and I feel his hand on my lower back.

I don't even realize I'm pressed against Zach, my fist clinging to the front of his Henley shirt. "I need to get to Harry at the monument. That's the only way to stop this," I tell him.

That's when I hear my name being called.

"Kat!"

"Katherine!"

"I love you, Kat Hadley!"

Descending on the green from the opposite direction of the Horseman are high school boys. Lots of them. I hear them calling my name while they move slowly as a pack as if they're paddling through mud. Reese, Hunter, and Justin are all there. So is Colton, cradling his head under his arm. But there are dozens more too.

"Oh no," I whimper.

"Are you threatening Kat?" Colton says, pointing at the Horseman.

His pumpkin head tilts like a curious puppy.

"She's our girl!" says Reese.

"Yeah, the best!" says another.

"We love you, Kat!" they chorus.

"And we'll save you!" Colton cries, and then the boys race forward, clashing spectacularly with the zombies.

So much for a damsel in distress. I'm going to have to rescue all of them—and fast.

"Zach!" I exclaim, an idea striking me as the clock finishes its twelfth chime. "Gather everyone you can and meet Harry and me at the monument! And hurry!"

Then I hold tight to my witch hat and dash off to the monument to reach Harry before it's too late.

28

Mystic Hollow Community Page

NEW POST FROM THE MYSTIC HOLLOW NEIGHBORHOOD WATCH: Lock your doors! Stay inside! The undead are here in Mystic Hollow!

NEW COMMENT FROM ANONYMOUS: LOL. Happy Halloween!

When I reach Harry at the monument, I see spell prep is well underway. She's drawn a circle with chalk and, instead of salt, she's painted a barrier using sugar packets from Witches Brew. The pentagram at the center of the circle could be blood, but it—

"Is that chocolate syrup?" I ask.

"I had to improvise," she grits out, paging through Beatrice's book. "That should be what it takes to end the Horseman. If we can do the wards—"

Behind us, I can hear the commotion on the green. People are shouting; several are screaming. I can't make out voices, but I'm worried for all of them. For Laney. For Zach. For all of us. The energy in the air is crackling with negativity. The wind picks up, and I take a deep breath. "Yes," I say, and reach for her hand. "Together."

"Together," she repeats, giving me an anxious smile. She loops Zach's apron, and I take the other end and do the same.

"Love that binds," I say. Because she's my sister. She'll be my sister forever.

"Love that finds," she repeats, holding up the donut. I almost laugh as we both lean in for a bite.

As the cakey sweet crumbles away, we lock hands and tighten the apron.

Right away, I feel the difference from the first time I cast this spell. The ground feels like it's settling, not cracking open again, and I feel a strange sense of peace. "I think it's working!" I say, hopeful, spitting donut on my sister's face. She frowns at me.

"We need more power. Our love isn't enough."

"It is," I tell her. "I know it is. You erased Jack's memories of your love, just to maybe save my heart."

Her smile trembles. "And you forgave me, even when I failed."

I grip her hand tighter. "I know you were just trying to be a good big sister. And I was just trying to measure up as your little sister. But we're more than our failures."

She clasps my hand right back. "We're sisters. And there's no love truer than that."

There's a blast of white light that extends from our hands and shoots up into the sky, arcing down across the entire town. Harry smiles at me. We've fixed the wards. She quickly kneels and scrabbles in the dirt at the base of the monument, burying the knot to seal the spell.

But then her smile falters. Because even once it's in the dirt, the Horseman is still coming, and his army of undead zombies is overcoming my army of lovesick boys.

"What do we do now?" she asks.

"A family makes a home," I say, thinking of Beatrice. "And you and I, we saved our home. But it takes a community to make a town."

"We're here!" Zach calls.

He's leading a large crowd of people our way with Laney at his side. There must be two hundred of them! I recognize several people from my party, Chris from Haunted House of Hamburgers. My teachers, the grocer, my neighbors. Mayor Croft and his wife are here too, and so is Laney's and Zach's werewolf guy/dog.

"I told everyone the Hadley sisters can't protect Mystic Hollow alone, and they all want to help," Zach explains.

"Mystic Hollow is nothing without the Hadleys!" Mayor Croft cries. He's wearing his traditional Halloween blazer, the one with the Headless Horseman on it in a checkered pattern that I'm certain after tonight he may never wear again. He looks around nervously. "Where are your aunts? And your mother?"

"It's just us, sir. And now all of you." I adjust the brim of my witch hat as the mayor looks at me nervously. The crowd murmurs to one another, and I can feel the fear radiating off them.

"Don't worry," Harry addresses everyone. "We're going to stop them, but everyone needs to listen."

"Where do you need us?" Laney asks.

"Everyone gather round the circle," I instruct them. "Don't step into it. Just gather round and hold hands. Quickly now!"

"He's coming!" someone cries, and everyone starts screaming.

Behind the crowd, I can see the Headless Horseman and his army advancing. My eyes lock with Zach's.

He nods. "You've got this, Hadley sisters!" a few others chime in.

"Go, Hadleys!" someone yells.

"Go, Kat, go!" Laney cheers as Ronald/Fred howls in agreement.

And then people start to cheer, their voices rising into the cloudless night.

"We aren't alone," I tell Harry, my heart thumping madly. My jitters fade away. How could I think I wasn't loved? My sister loves me. My family loves me. And my town loves me. "Let's finish this together. All of us."

"All of us," Harry agrees. "Everyone, get ready!"

People get into position, the circle growing larger and larger as people take each other's hands. Harry and I are the only two not part of it yet. With a nod, Harry flicks on another match and ignites the monument. The stone shouldn't catch, but with magic it does, the marble melting like butter in the sun. We're sacrificing the town monument for the town. I feel my magic tingling, working along with the spell.

"I think it's working now!" I yell to Harry over the roar of the crowd, people cheering and yelling our names.

"The sacrifice is done," Harry says, clutching Beatrice's spell book again. "Now we just need the intention. Everyone! Repeat after us: *This circle is cast, protect Mystic Hollow at last.* Say it over and over again till we tell you to stop. Got it?"

"Yes! Yes! Hurry! The Horseman is almost here!" the mayor says.

Harry and I rejoin the circle and begin to chant along with the others. I clasp hands with Harry and with Zach, and feel my magic surge under my skin. A small crackle of energy and a light that begins to glow from within. *It's working!* I want to cry, but just as it starts to pulse, I feel it fade away again. Something is wrong. Is our love not enough? Just when I'm ready to fear the worst, there is a large pop and a massive gust of wind.

A vortex of swirling light appears like a cloud, and I can see through it to another space and time. Into a . . . ballroom?

And then Aunt Viv and Aunt Diane step out, decked from head to toe in the sparkliest formal wear.

"Aunt Viv!" I cry, wanting to break from the circle. "Aunt Diane!"

"Girls! Oh, thank the stars!" Aunt Diane says, looking misty.

Aunt Viv looks from us to the crowd, then to the Horseman's army, inching closer. "I see we made it just in time." She muscles into the circle beside the mayor. "Croft? Give me your hand. Get in here, Diane!"

As soon as they join us, I can feel the difference in our magic immediately. Mine is pulsing now, the energy in our joined hands growing big and bigger before a bright white light forms over our massive circle. And still, we keep chanting, until finally there is a blast that sends waves of energy over the circle with such force, we're knocked to the ground. Every light gutters, the scarecrows and the torches, the jack-o'-lanterns—even the poop one.

And then comes the wind, a screaming gale.

"Don't let go!" my aunts scream, and we all hold each other's hands tighter.

The wind forms a cyclone, whipping up first the gnomes and the gremlins, then the vampires, the werewolves, the kraken. Finally, only the Horseman stands, a few yards away.

He doesn't need a face to convey his rage.

He raises his gloved finger, points it at me, and kicks his steed into a gallop.

"Kat!" my sister yells, trying to yank me away, as the Horseman's mount leaps up, black hooves flashing.

I squeeze my eyes shut, clinging to my sister.

"Oh stars," I hear my aunts whisper.

I open my eyes slowly to the stone-white hoof of a horse statue. Atop it sits a headless figure, axe raised, finger pointing straight at me.

29

Mystic Hollow Community Page

NEW POST FROM MAYOR CROFT: Dear Citizens, we have much to celebrate thanks to the Hadley girls. Cleanup will continue throughout the weekend. Just remember: What happens in Mystic Hollow stays in Mystic Hollow. Have a great time!

"I don't remember Great-Aunt Aida's portrait looking so cheerful," Harry says as she lifts the mended painting off the floor and places it back on the wall.

I walk over, broom in hand, to look at it myself. The drab oil painting has definitely changed. Sun is streaming through the window behind Aida, and her dress has gone from brown to a pretty mauve. "I think she's actually smiling now."

"I, for one, was sick of her scowl," says Aunt Diane as she uses magic to move a few vases and knickknacks. They float through the air and return to their regular places. "Apparently, she was too."

"Mom's going to notice," Harry and I say in unison, then look at each other. "Jinx!" Phoebe winds her way around both of our legs, meowing happily.

"Your mom will not notice. She'll just be happy you two made up," Aunt Viv insists as she waltzes by, spelling things here and there to make sure everything in the house is back to normal.

I've been concentrating on the wallpaper that peeled in the dining room, imbuing glue with my magic, and slowly and surely the walls have returned to their normal selves as well. My aunts and Harry can't stop talking about how impressed they are with my magic skills. I know I still have a long way to go, but it feels good to understand my own magic now and know that while it hasn't manifested in the same way as the other Hadleys, it's just as strong.

We've worked hard together to use magic to fix what was broken. Colton's head is firmly back on his body. The ice realm is gone. The dead have returned to their resting places. The greenhouse is accessible again too. This morning, I checked on Victor, and the Venus flytrap is back to his normal size. He was happy to hear me sing "Monster Mash" to him again. Harry's magic is working once more, and she was able to charm her hair into cooperating again. And as for me? Every boy who confessed their dying love to me is back to ignoring me. A day later, all is back to normal. *Almost.*

I feel a rush of cold air on my neck. "I came to say my goodbyes," says Eleanor, floating through a wall to greet us.

"I wish I could stay and see your parents, but my sister is expecting me."

"I'm so glad you've made your peace with everything and are moving on," I tell her. "We're going to miss you though."

"Maybe we will all join you for Samhain next year when the veil thins," Eleanor says brightly, clasping her hands together. "She's going to love hearing about the creature in the sink."

Aunt Diane pops her head around a corner. "Sink? Oh, girls, please tell me there wasn't a slimy tentacle in the same spot where I wash my coffee cup."

"It's gone now," I remind her. "It's like it never happened at all."

"I wouldn't exactly say *that*," says Aunt Viv, placing *A Guide to Your Magic* back in my hands and handing Harry a copy as well. "I'd say you both had a hell of a crash course in magic."

"Believe me, we know, Aunt Viv," says Harry as she touches the new crystal necklace around her neck.

Aunt Viv and Aunt Diane got us new ones as soon as they heard what we did with the originals.

"And now we know, the rituals can be cast by any sort of love. We don't need boys."

The aunts trade a look. "That's what we've been saying for years," Aunt Diane mutters dryly.

"And we know," Harry continues, "that sisterhood is its own kind of magic. It requires sacrifice—and intention."

"Thank the stars! My work here is done!" Eleanor says as she begins to fade from view.

We stare for a moment at where she stood, but then Harry disappears into the basement. "I found this earlier, when I was checking the foundation. Think we should hang it up?"

It's a portrait of Eleanor—and her sister.

"Yeah," I say, my throat tight. "We should."

She smiles, affixing it the wall. "I hope Mom and Dad are home soon," Harry says. "I have to catch a train back to school."

"We're going to miss you," I say. "Really."

"You don't have to miss me because you are going to visit next weekend, and then Thanksgiving is right around the corner," Harry says. "I can't miss Mayor Croft running the Turkey Trot in a turkey costume. Did you hear him say he's going to make Mystic Hollow the number one destination for Thanksgiving?"

We both laugh.

"And I decided something," Harry tells all of us. "I'm going to relax more. Not worry about grades so much."

Aunt Viv feels her head. "No fever. Are you all right?"

"I'm fine," Harry says, and looks at me knowingly. "I guess I've just realized it's not a competition. I have to figure out what I want to do, otherwise there's nothing to be gained from winning."

"Except the trophy?" I joke. But really I'm proud of her,

and I know I could learn a lot from this lesson too. I'm not saying I don't want to beat Zach to be valedictorian next year or get into the college of my dreams, whatever that is, but I don't have to be so focused on being perfect. No one is. "Does that mean you'll let me beat you at Monopoly?"

Before Harry can answer, we all hear the front door creaking open.

The four of us look at each other, as if we've just been caught out. Aunt Viv and Aunt Diane agree that the less Mom and Dad know about what happened the better. How we can keep it a secret when the whole town was there with us is beyond me, but the aunts said not to worry. Here's hoping they're right.

I take a nervous glance around the first floor to be sure everything other than Great-Aunt Aida's portrait is back to normal as my parents wheel their bags down the front hall. The four of us stand at attention, like a welcome party.

"We're home!" Mom declares as she steps into the living room. She sees my aunts and stops short. "What are you two doing here? Why aren't you on the cruise?"

"Hi!" Harry and I say, rushing forward to hug them. Then Aunt Viv and Aunt Diane pile in too, and we're all talking a mile a minute, my aunts explaining that they've realized they hate cruising (lie—although maybe true for this cruise, since my bad spell accidentally sent them to the Bermuda Triangle), and my uncles decided to take the six-month cruise instead. They don't want to miss the next Broadway season anyway. Then we rush them into the kitchen, where we've got a fresh apple crisp waiting.

"Ooh! You girls are so sweet. We haven't eaten all morning," Mom says, grabbing a spoonful and plopping down at the island alongside Dad to have some. "Are these from Mystic Hollow Apple Orchard?"

"Yep," I tell them, feeling slightly anxious as I eye Mom's favorite milk pitcher on the shelf behind her that the yeti smashed and I did a spell to fix. I hope she doesn't notice. Or anything else we had to mend in her favorite room of the house. "We picked them up this morning to make you the crisp as a welcome home present."

"Aren't you sweet, girls," Dad says, and his eyes fill up with tears. "We missed you! I hated doing Samhain without you all."

Mom sighs. "I had the strangest sensation that I was needed, but then when midnight came, I felt more settled and knew everything was well."

Harry and I look at one another as Aunt Viv pours tea and the teacup stirs itself with a spoon. "I can honestly say it brought us closer together," I say.

"I couldn't agree more," Harry agrees.

"How is Grams?" I ask. "And Grampa?"

"They're good, Kitty Kat," Dad says. "They miss you both and are going to join us for Samhain next year for sure."

"We can do the rituals with Grams. Together."

Mom looks at us curiously. "So where did you bury the

rope? I want to add Grams's and mine to the site to strengthen the magic even more."

"You didn't bury yours?" I ask, panic flaring.

"You're supposed to," Harry adds, sounding equally nervous. "I thought they needed to go in dirt immediately."

"They did," Dad says, pulling a Ziploc bag of dirt out of his carry-on bag and holding it up proudly before staring lovingly at my mom. "Your mother is the best witch I know."

Mom wipes her mouth with a napkin and stands up. "You are too sweet, my love. Let's take care of that now. So where is the hole?" Mom asks.

My aunts, Harry, and I look at each other.

"For that, dear sister, we need to take a field trip," Aunt Viv says. "We buried the knots at the Croft monument in town."

"Why would you do that?" Mom asks. "We always do the rituals here at the house."

"Well, this year," Aunt Diane says, her eyes flashing in my direction, "Kat and Harry helped us realize there is always room for spell improvement."

"But . . . in the center of town? Where everyone can see?" Mom asks, confused.

Mom looks at me and I realize there is no point denying this part. I glance Harry's way and she nods in agreement, as if she's heard my thoughts. "Yep! Why don't we show you?"

30

Mystic Hollow Community Page

NEW POST FROM JACKIE ROGERS: It's November 1st! Halloween is over! When are you taking down your decorations, people?

"I don't know why we never thought to do this before," Mom marvels as we stand in front of the restored Harold Croft monument in the center of the town square a short while later.

It's close to dinnertime and dusk is settling over Mystic Hollow, giving the town the best of magical feels with a sky that is popping with autumnal colors.

"I can feel the magic here in a way I actually don't in the house," Mom continues. "You girls are right. This must be the point in town where magic is the strongest with Beatrice's spell book here. It's the beating heart of our town. With all this love for Mystic Hollow . . . it's perfect."

"It was Kat's idea," Harry says as she pulls her green

sweater tightly around her body to block the breeze. "When she suggested it, I was like, how can I refuse when she's so right?" Harry grins mischievously at me.

"Sweetheart, I'm so proud of you," Mom says to me as Dad grabs a trowel and begins digging in the spot we told him to.

The aunts restored the base to its original design with one improvement—a panel that will pop out if we ever need to reach Beatrice's spell book again.

I sink into her hug, happy for the praise, while my eyes are still on my sister. "Well, I couldn't have done it without Harry." The two of us wink.

It's a perfect fall afternoon. The green is packed with people enjoying the weather, and that includes droves of tourists. I've heard that the leaf-peeping tours have sold out for the rest of the year; the carnival has extended its stay, and lines snake all the way from the school parking lot to the green. And Witches Brew has been a madhouse, so packed I haven't even tried to set foot inside.

Well, that, and I'm scared of running into Zach. I'm scared of how he'll treat me, now that magic was fixed. My sister undid her spell with help from the aunts, who are experts at undoing magic, and she told me she's going to reach out to Jack and see if he remembers. Now I'm not a boy magnet or completely invisible.

I'm just Kat.

And I'm looking forward to figuring out who that is—without boys.

"Hey, Kat!"

I look up and see Colton running by with some friends to play a game of flag football on the green.

"Hey, Kat!" the other guys say in unison.

"Hey!" I wave and smile. Do any of them remember being an army of Kat Hadley lovers? I'm not sure. The aunts claim when the magic boundaries were restored, all went back to the way it was. Well, except one thing.

"Girls? Was there always a monument to the Headless Horseman in the green?" Mom asks, walking a few feet away to marvel at the massive stone structure of the Horseman on a skeleton horse, his sword raised high, the horse rearing back on two legs, pawing the air.

"Yes," we all agree at once.

"How do you not remember?" Aunt Viv asks. "It's been there since 1645."

"Really?" Mom frowns. "I guess I never walk through the green, just around it."

"The knots are buried," Dad says, wiping his hands. "Who wants to celebrate another successful Samhain with a coffee at Witches Brew?"

My stomach drops.

We walk over together; everyone in the family talking at once, giving their orders, and their preferences for caffeinated or decaffeinated beverages. I can hear the pumpkin-carving tool revving from across the green. There's going to be no avoiding Zach, and I still feel a bit funny about our conversation last night. Will he remember me saying I wanted to kiss him?

I feel a tingling and look up to see Harry staring at me intently. *I've got you*, she seems to say, and I wonder if that's my magic coming in, if I'll be able to hear her thoughts.

"Kat is going to get the orders, and we're going to stay here and hang out by Beatrice's spell book since she's family," Harry tells them, shepherding my parents back toward the monument. Aunt Viv suddenly has a picnic blanket and a cheese board out of nowhere, and the group settles in as Harry squeezes my hand and whispers in my ear, "You've got this."

I cross the quad, watching the line of people outside Witches Brew as I approach. It must be twenty people deep, but I've never had to wait in line here. Standing there is torture; I have so much time to imagine how Zach will look at me, or how he won't look at me. When I make it to the coffee shop, my heart is beating in my chest as I try to think about what I'm going to say when I see Zach. Instead, barking interrupts my thoughts, and the next thing I know, giant muddy paws are clawing at my skirt.

"Ronald Frederick!" I hear Laney command. "Get down!" She rushes over and clips a leash onto him. I see the black dog has a dog tag with his two names on it. "Sorry, Kat. He was much better behaved as a boy," she grumbles, though she's petting his head. "I still can't believe I fell for him. I should have known when he tried to lick my face!" I can't help but giggle. "It's not funny!" Laney yells at me before she dissolves into laughter too. "When am I going to meet a normal boy? Are there any that even exist in Mystic Hollow?"

I see Zach at the window out of the corner of my eye. "Normal is overrated." I lean down and pat Ronald/Fred. "What's with the collar? Did you adopt him?"

"Ugh, no," Laney says, and brushes a strand of hair behind her right ear, revealing turkey dangling earrings. "Zach did, but he agreed I can take him on walks when Witches Brew is busy." Laney smirks. "Did you know having a dog is a great way to meet boys?"

I laugh. "I didn't."

"Seriously, I've talked to three guys from school already that I've never spoken to before."

"Since when were you so boy obsessed?" I ask Laney. "Let's just enjoy being single. We have each other."

Zach emerges from the side door of Witches Brew, carrying a tray of pumpkin spice lattes in pumpkins. When he sees me, my stomach starts doing that strange fluttering thing again and my magic tingles excitedly. Laney sees me and Zach looking at each other.

"You do have me. But that doesn't mean you have to be single."

"What?"

She smiles. "I'm going to take Ronald Frederick on his

third walk of the afternoon. Text me later!" With that, Ronald takes off at a run, pulling Laney out to the green.

"Hey," Zach says, putting the drinks down at a nearby table.

"Hey," I manage. My palms are sweating, my fingers shaking. My magic sweeps through me like a warm wave as he approaches. Zach is way cuter than I ever gave him credit for. Has any boy ever worn a Henley as well as he does? Or had such full lips? Lips I want to kiss? *Say something, Kat*, I think. "I . . ." I start to say, but there's no need, because Zach says everything I need to hear.

"I've been thinking about what you said last night . . . about wanting to kiss me."

"You have?" I say, my face burning as the speaker at the coffee shop seems to kick into overdrive, blasting a mellow Taylor Swift tune that is perfect for dusk and moonlit nights like this one is about to be. In the distance, I think I hear a howl. Maybe it's Ronald. Maybe the werewolves are back. But at the moment, I don't care. "And what do you think about that?" I say breathlessly.

"I think it's a really good idea," Zach says as he wraps his arms around my waist and lifts me into the air before his lips are on mine. And it is pure magic.

Acknowledgments

For the past twenty years, I've had a standing October date with my friend Miana Delucia to drop everything we have going on in life and watch *Practical Magic* together. We've never missed a viewing, and I think that's why I have always associated fall with this movie I love so much. So imagine my delight when editor Sara Schonfeld offered me the chance to tell a story about two witchy sisters in a small town who have their own brush with broken spells and accidental magic the week leading up to Halloween. Sara, I have loved getting to work on this story with you. I am so thankful for your insight, guidance, and hand-holding as we worked at lightning speed to make this story a reality.

As always, there are so many people who come together to make a book possible. Thank you to Claire Callahan, Amanda Maciel, Erica Sussman, and the rest of the editorial team that helped me tell this story. To Kelley McMorris and Jessie Gang, who created a cover I am so in love with, I show it to everyone like a proud mom. And to Mary Magrisso, Erin DeWitt, Erika West, Heather Tamarkin, Annabelle Sinoff, and everyone else at Harper who helped turn my story into a book.

My agent, Dan Mandel, who knew there was no way I could say no to this story once it took hold and did his own sort of magic to make it possible for me to write this. And my husband and children, who were so patient when it felt like I was on deadline for the entire fall (probably because I was).

Finally, to the readers who have been with me since day one and keep coming back to hear new stories. I'm so thankful you've taken a chance on this story about Kat and Harry, and the power of magic, sisterhood, and love.